Sto

PETRUS

Dog of the Hill Country

Time and again they thrust down upon her

PETRUS

Dog of the Hill Country

BY

JOSEPH E. CHIPPERFIELD

ILLUSTRATED BY

STUART TRESILIAN

DAVID McKAY COMPANY, INC.

NEW YORK

PETRUS

First Edition November 1960
Reprinted November 1962

LIBRARY OF CONGRESS CATALOG CARD NUMBER 60-13341

Printed in the United States of America

Dedication

*For all those
whose humanity is directed toward
the preservation of animals
and to*

MISS WINIFRED FRENCH

*of Bookham, Surrey,
whose devotion to dogs,
and to Alsatians in particular,
makes me proud to be
numbered amongst her friends.*

Contents

Illustrations

PART ONE

Dog of the Hill Country

1: The Hill Called Hebron

THE HILL stood a long way off, bleak and desolate. A gray mist hid the lower slopes, for the rains had come early that year. Instead of the occasional shower during the ninth month, it had already rained more days than it was fine, and by the tenth month, the rainy season was well established over the heights of Judaea, and the hill was scarcely visible from the great Sea of the Plain where the humidity lay like a blanket along the entire western shore.

No more featureless area could be found in the whole of Judaea than that east of the central range of hills that formed the backbone of the entire country from Beersheba in the south to Samaria in the north. It was little better than salt marshland flanking the tideless wastes of the Dead Sea that lay in the vast volcanic depression extending for some forty miles.

To the weary, half-savage animal that traveled the steaming saltlands, it was a sure refuge from those she had deserted to join up with a wild dog from the hill caves. Even so, she kept glancing uneasily over her shoulder as she loped along. The grim fate that had overtaken her lawless companion was an oft-recurring memory. He had attempted a raid of the very flock she had not long since guarded, and had been discovered by the shepherds. They, with determination, had set off to trail the dog to his lair.

The shepherd bitch and her wild mate

The lair was high in one of the many limestone caves that, in more ancient days, had been the burial caves of the Edomites. It was early in the morning when the wild dog came scrambling up to the den with the remains of a lamb hanging from his drooling jaws. The shepherd bitch heard him approaching and ran out to greet him. Whining with pleasure, she failed to notice far down the hillside those who had once been her masters.

Both animals were feasting on the lamb when the shepherds fell upon them, killing the wild dog with one thrust of a crook used in the herding of sheep. The renegade animal managed to leap away in time to save herself and fled up into the hills. Following a well-defined watercourse she did not come down again into the plains by the inland sea until three days had come and gone, and no trace of the shepherds remained to bring fear into her heart.

She then set off southward, keeping close to the shores of the Dead Sea and traveled as far from her old home as she could. By deserting the flock and joining up with the wild dog, she knew that she had become an outcast. Thus she pressed on nervously, and finding nothing in the plain to sustain her, she soon grew lean and red-eyed with hunger. Scarcely a thing lived by the Sea of the Plain, and save where a spring burst out from some hidden source, the low-lying marshland contained little in the way of vegetation.

There was, however, some form of wild life up in the limestone cliffs — birds for the most part.

The marauding animal soon became aware of them — vultures that ceaselessly encircled her and sent raucous cries echoing across the tideless sea.

This Ishmael of the canine race was not long in doubt as to their intentions. Time and time again they thrust down upon her, sending her stumbling, and even on one occasion essaying a direct attack upon her. She sensed what would happen if she did not soon leave this place of desolation. Her bones would whiten the shores of the very sea that, in a past age, had seen other bones piled up about it as the Cities of the Plain in their wickedness fell before the scourge of fire from heaven.

The animal was growing steadily weaker and more and more apprehensive as she continued her lone journey onward, finally striking off in the direction of the hill country and the ancient mountain height that seemed to draw her and yet seemed so very far away.

There was desperation in her as she followed a watercourse, for soon she must find a refuge for herself that was safe in surroundings where a little hunting would help to provide for those she would shortly bring into the world.

Toward nightfall, on the eleventh day of her journeying she found a withering cypress still clinging to a rock crevasse. It was a weird sight — the half-dead tree, rooted firmly in the living rock. Even as she reached it, she could hear a frail whimpering of the stray breezes that continually swept the slope.

She was now in dire need of rest, and there was a stream of clear water near by. She first drank greedily, and then the truant shepherd bitch stretched herself out to full length, her hind legs extended to ease the aching muscles.

Her hunger was great, her exhaustion also. Yet a sudden movement from under the cypress brought her stumbling to her feet — a new vitality flowed into her limbs as a brown-furred creature raced away from her with a whisk of its scut. In three quick leaps, she was upon the small creature, who died the very instant her fangs closed over its neck.

The food — the first she had tasted for many days — put strength into her body, and after a long rest under the withered tree, she resumed her hunting, and was rewarded by yet another easy kill.

By noon the following day, she had recovered sufficiently to continue her trek up into the hill country. More vital than ever now was her need for a satisfactory lair until her hour was fulfilled, but it seemed that though the birds of the air had nests and the beasts of the hill country their own secret dens, for her — an outcast from her own kind — there was no place to give her covering.

The rain, like a breath of mist, was sweeping high over the heights of Hebron, but down on the terraced slopes it was the stuff of which streams are formed, and the distressed animal was ofttimes blinded by it. She pressed on only because of the urgency of her need to find shelter up among the crags where man was unlikely to come.

At last, the summit of the Hill of Hebron was less than a mile away. It rose out of the rain like a rounded cone, pitted in places where caves abounded. There many another creature had found refuge.

Her greatest problem now was to find a home. Backward and forward she went, using her nose as never before. Every gully, every outcrop, she investigated thoroughly, but without avail.

Then when it seemed this lonely mountain height, too,

would fail her, she came upon a cairn of stones with a tunnel slanting in toward the center. Sniffing eagerly, she crawled down into the darkness, and discovered a sizeable cave. What was most important to her, it was lined with dry moss.

For an hour or more, she lay panting quietly, listening for any stray sound, finally accepting that she had indeed found a lair that nobody owned, although her nose told her only too strongly it had been occupied by a hill fox who had been none too particular. Decayed rubbish offended her nostrils until she busied herself in tidying up the den.

That night, she hunted with determination so that she could provide for her young when they were born. Soon, she had food a-plenty stored in the recesses of the cave, and she then relaxed, awaiting her hour.

The next day was humid, with scarcely a breath of air moving on the summit height. Late in the afternoon, the shepherd bitch lay near the entrance of the lair, her nose constantly testing the atmosphere. She had some doubts as to the identities of her neighbors since they were, for the most part, nocturnal hunters. She used her nose to warn her should any attack be contemplated by one or other of them.

Being so long the helpmate of man, she had no real knowledge of the ways of the wild, having been with the hill dog, her mate, for so short a period. Even so, short though that time had been, she had learned one thing from him — not to trust blindly other creatures she might encounter. Now, because of those whom soon she would have to rear in the uncompromising world of the mountain, she was more than unduly suspicious.

Moreover, she had discovered that wild boars hunted

along the western slope of the mountain, and she had no desire to make their acquaintance.

All that afternoon as she lay with head close to the entrance to the lair, she could hear their distant quarreling and grunting, and sensed instinctively that of all animals of the wild, the boar was the one to be feared the most.

Toward evening there was a distinct change in the direction of the intermittent breeze. The heavy atmosphere was lifting a little, and the drift of rain and mist was less apparent over the mountain. Then, as so often happened in that central area of hills where the climate changed with bewildering rapidity from frigid to torrid, the entire central highland range began to emerge and take on definite shape. It became much cooler, and a hill bird called out, loud and clear.

The listening animal, gasping from the oppressive atmosphere of the cave, ventured farther into the open, lying half in and half out of the lair, panting with sudden pleasure.

She must have lain thus for the best part of an hour while the knowledge of her destiny moved uncertainly in the depths of her being. No strong memory had she any longer of the wild dog for whom she had deserted the campfires of the shepherds; no memory either of the shepherd she had known as her own particular master.

All that had happened to her during her sojourn with the sheep herds was not even a faint echo in her consciousness, and only in rare moments did she seem to hear the movement of sheep under a night sky, and see, like a mirage afar off, the flickering glow of a campfire before which sat men, whom she had once obeyed.

But that call of the wild dog to which she had responded seemed to come to her now as she lay quiet and at ease. Faint but unmistakable in its meaning, the call seemed to wind out from some hidden fastness of the Hill of Hebron . . . winding down like a note blown from an instrument fashioned of horn such as she had seen the shepherds use.

Suddenly she became taut with terror. The call, if call indeed it was, was louder now, more insistent.

Then it was no more, and in the silence that followed, the shepherd bitch could feel the heavy pounding of her heart with fear. Her nose searched the air streams; her eyes stared away over the undulating ridge of the highland that overlooked the great Sea of the Plain — that dead sea where nothing lived.

Suddenly she was on her feet, trembling with anxiety. It had been no real call she had heard, coming down to her from some distant place . . . only an instinctive warning in her own mind.

As she turned about and went scrambling into the security of the den, the hoarse grunt of a boar was heard, and a tusked animal lumbered into sight, pausing for a few moments less than five yards away. He then proceeded toward the western slopes of Mount Hebron, where the hunting was always to his liking.

For a very long time after his departure, the shepherd bitch lay motionless, her ears pricked for any sign of his return. It continued quiet, and the slow-passing hours fell into the gloom of night.

Twice — thrice, perhaps, the hill bird called from way over the shoulder of the mountain. Of the boar, however, no sound at all. It was so quiet, so very quiet on that hill called Hebron.

The hour of the shepherd bitch came at last when a new moon stood high over the Sea of the Plain and the last of the rain went drifting away across the heights of Moab.

The birds of the air had nests; those animals of the wild their sheltering crevasses and rocks, and she — an Ishmael of her kind — a lair at last. A rank den, in very truth, where a fox had once dwelt, still, a lair and a covering from the dangers of the hill; and there she brought forth her young, and among them one who, one day, would be known as Petrus — the dog who never grew old.

2: The World of the Wild

DAWN WAS but a tentative overture above Mount Hebron, lasting no more than a few short minutes. Then — since the rain had completely died out during the hours of darkness — the sun came up, strident like the blast of many trumpets sounding in the blue arc of the sky. Glowing, it caused the saltlands adjacent to the Sea of the Plain to steam with vapor, and the highlands above it to shimmer in a heat haze.

It was very quiet in the lair where the shepherd bitch lay with her puppies pressed close against her. There were five of them — four females and one male. Not one of them could be termed robust, for their mother had traveled too great a distance before they had been born, and had endured too long a period of privation.

Disappointing though they might be to her, with the feel of their tiny bodies close against her, the mother was determined to do her best to rear them. She nuzzled them tenderly as they whimpered in their sleep, letting her tongue pass over them gently.

Outside on the mountain, the wild boars continued to grunt and quarrel, and at the distant sounds, the shepherd bitch would gather the puppies closer to her, panting with anxiety and never relaxing until the sounds had died away and it was quiet again.

Slowly the days passed; the rainy season lost much of its severity and down in the fertile plains, husbandmen were planting their seeds and attending to many occupations so there might be a good harvest when the time came.

The puppies grew and seemed to thrive in that dark cave under the cairn. Their mother was tireless in attending to their many wants, and hunted with great cunning so that fresh food would always be available to satisfy their voracious appetites. At the back of her mind was the hope that she might thus give them the strength they must assuredly possess if they were to survive on the hill where so many struggled and died, and only the strongest remained.

She was not long in becoming aware of the male puppy. He was not only the strongest, but also the most mischievous. He romped and played in the confines of the lair, and often, when his mother was absent on some hunting expedition, he would venture to the tunnel mouth, intrigued by the blaze of golden light that streamed down comforting warmth.

Somehow he sensed that if he could but summon up sufficient courage and push his way through that wall of light, he would find beyond it that mysterious place his mother visited so frequently.

His young eyes, so recently opened, were only accustomed to the gloom of the lair, and the dazzle of the sunglow at the mouth of the tunnel, while attracting him, yet kept him at a respectful distance by reason of its intensity.

Then one evening when the glow was no longer there, but a half-light alone cast a screen at the top of the tunnel, the shepherd bitch herself caught up the puppies one by one, and took them to the tunnel mouth, and passing through that strange radiance, set them side by side on a sandy slope that was sheltered by the uprising cairn of stones.

This was their first experience of the outside world, and what a curious world it was. The light was fast dying away in the west, and stars, like huge lamps, seemed suspended high above the mountain. More important than the stars, however, was the immense shield of burnished gold coming up out of the east. For a very long time, the puppies lay quietly looking upward, while low down on the horizon, more and more stars made their appearance and the full moon soared high over the mountain range.

It was not until the night bird uttered his warning cry on the western slopes that the shepherd bitch drove her puppies back into the tunnel under the cairn.

That first sight of moon and stars remained with them for a long time, and even in sleep, more than one of the small family seemed to be reliving the experience.

More such nights were granted them by their mother, then the moon was no longer there in the sky, only the stars. In the darkness, each puppy could hear the swift pounding of a heart suddenly apprehensive because of the gloom. Thus did they begin to learn the meaning of fear, and with it the extreme need for caution. For them, in their inexperience, fear and caution seemed to go hand in hand.

The shepherd bitch, an alien in the world of the wild, was trying her utmost to teach the puppies how to survive and avoid all possible dangers. Moreover, her own apprehension was often so communicated to them that they were sent stumbling into the tunnel, where they lay waiting for some sign from her before emerging again.

In this, if not in anything else, their education was proceeding on satisfactory lines, and in some obscure way, their mother was content. Not many days later, she began to plan wider and more exciting excursions on the hill, quickly followed by first lessons in hunting.

It was not long then before she sensed that life on Mount Hebron was fast assuming a pattern that she could understand and appreciate because of its age-old familiarity. She started to lose her fears, and with them, a little of her hereditary caution. She even began to forget that there were wild boars forever hunting on the western slopes of the mountain.

Indeed, life was now of such quietude that she slept free from anxiety, and her puppies continued to thrive in an atmosphere of calm.

Then once again there was a new moon rising up out of the great Sea of the Plain; in no time, it was a yellow half-moon — then a full moon, bronze like the shields of the Roman conquerors.

On the last night of the full moon, the wild boars went hunting.

The boars were hunting singly. A couple were questing along the main ridge, each moving more than half a mile from the other. Two more, adopting the same tactics, were quartering the ground a little south of the cairn. For once the animals were silent, and their individual activities could only be determined by a stain in the wind. As their excitement grew, so did the scent become stronger. It remained long in the air streams, warning all other creatures of their presence.

Within a second of leaving the lair, the shepherd bitch was warned of their activities. Returning to the tunnel she lay for some time motionless, and did not attempt to leave again until she was assured that all the puppies were sleeping.

Once again on the hilltop, she stood testing the air currents, and was aware of being perplexed, for with every change of breeze she got some warning of the boars' presence, but found it difficult to tell exactly where they were. Then quite suddenly she realized that almost every member of the boar family was abroad that night, and the danger from some chance encounter was greatly increased.

It was a lovely night, quiet as only a night could be when everything on the mountain lay still and expectant.

The moon, large and honey-colored, rose steadily out of the hill country beyond the Sea of the Plain. Rocks and the downward fall of the mountain slopes stood out in sharp relief, with every cypress and bush rising distorted.

An hour or so after the moon had risen, the shepherd bitch wandered along the ridge, with ears keenly erect and hearing nothing but the heavy pounding of her own heart. She was still apprehensive, for the scent of the boars remained a tingling stain on the constantly veering air currents.

After a while, she decided to leave the ridge and investigate the surrounding area. She moved silently, little more than a shadow in the amber spilling of the moonlight. Her body was low to the ground as she loped along, her tail tucked between her legs.

She came unexpectedly upon the spoor of one of the boars, and halted bristling, while a low growl sounded in her throat. The scent was warm, but no sound of the creature could she hear. Once again she tested the air currents, then having satisfied herself as to the direction that would be safest, she turned slightly southward. She made an encircling trek, rejoining the ridge a mile or so from its highest point.

It was then she came upon the second of the boars. The creature had made a kill, and was feasting with grunts of satisfaction.

Tense with shock, the shepherd bitch stood a little distance away watching him. Then, as silently as she had appeared, she swung about, and again made another detour, this time joining the ridge where it dipped down toward a series of hummocks.

Here she intended doing her hunting, and because there was no scent in the air to warn her, she set about her quest with no idea that a boar lay in waiting amongst the hummocky slopes.

The awesome stench of the boar came to her suddenly. In a moment, she forgot all else in a rising surge of fear, and took refuge behind one of the hummocks, every hair on her back and neck bristling, her lips drawn back in a silent snarl.

Despite her great fear, she was prepared to fight with all the tenacity of her kind. Not only for her own life did she tense her muscles for the stand she must make against the most dreaded enemy on the Hill of Hebron. There were also her puppies who still needed her to hunt for them.

As a vague memory of the puppies stirred in the depths of her consciousness, and with it, some fleeting impression of the wild dog who had been her mate, the snarl wrinkling her muzzle became more terrifying. For an instant, she felt she was no longer alone, and that the shadow of her mate stood by her side.

The moon swung up behind her, and the defile in which she stood apprehensively alert became filled with the overspill of its amber light.

Meanwhile, the boar, more cunning than she, had moved silently to the rear of the hummock, and in a second or two, had taken up a position of advantage on the crest.

The shepherd bitch was completely unaware of the danger that threatened her from the rear, the indifferent wind again failing her when most she needed its assistance.

Then, perhaps, for one chaotic second did she become conscious of the fate about to overtake her — one instant in which her heart seemed no longer to beat and her eyes, in a quick backward glance, caught and held the impression of the tusked shape already crouched to leap on her.

Sharp amongst the many impressions transmitted to her brain in that last moment was the bronze shield of the moon. Perhaps in her great travail she was blinded by it and did not see the tusked shape bearing down upon her. Then the night and the moon were taken from her eyes, and she went forth to join the lawless spirit of her mate.

An hour later, the hollow was silent and deserted, and

the amber overflow of moonlight now fell on a ridge of uprising ground so that heavy shadows darkened the arena
where death had raised a beckoning finger and passed
on. . . .

3: The Inhospitable Hill

THAT NIGHT in the lives of the shepherd puppies, now unprotected in the lair on the Hill of Hebron, was long in passing. While they slept, massed together for warmth since it grew cold toward dawn, the moonlight outside grew dim, and the night shadows deepened. No more did the night bird call over the solitary wastes, nor the wild boars grunt. It had become very silent. Not even the rustle of the rising breeze possessed sufficient voice to penetrate the lair, and found but little to toss in its path save perhaps a few tufts of hair which, but a few hours before, had been shed by the shepherd bitch who had met her end in a hollow where now the darkest of shadows concealed her mutilated shape.

The motherless puppies slept long, and dawn had, a good hour since, fluttered its banners of crimson and gold over the hill when the first of them awakened and opened an inquisitive eye before yawning.

It was the male puppy, and he lay very still for a few seconds listening intently, while his nose constantly tested the air streams filtering down from the opening under the cairn. Then he became aware of being hungry, and was puzzled not to find his mother in her accustomed place, keeping her watch over that shaft that thrust upward to the outside world.

The beam of sunlight striking down through the opening became stronger. It was a very bright day outside, and the puppy decided to go to the top of the shaft and investigate. He was no longer afraid to thrust himself through the wall of opaque light to reach the cherished play spot. His mother had long since destroyed the illusion that neither he nor his sisters could leave the lair without her assistance.

One of the sleeping puppies whimpered as he moved away; one cried out as he accidentally trod on her as he scrambled up the tunnel. A second later and he crouched at the opening, staring out. The sunshine lay warm and golden upon the rocks and upon the sparse grass that went in undulating waves toward the rim of the hill where it dipped down to join the main ridge.

The breeze was still flowing over the escarpment like a lost thing seeking something to shape it into a steady current of air. Once again it brought the illusion of life to the tufts of hair, and the puppy, bristling for a moment with fear, felt moved to leave the security of the cairn to sniff what he readily recognized as something belonging to his mother.

Her scent lay all about him. Young though he was, the instinctive use of his nose told him that she had gone off along the ridge, but because he sensed that it was a long way from the lair, he did not attempt to follow his mother's spoor. Within a few seconds, he had returned to the cave under the cairn of stones where he lay watching and waiting.

He had no idea of time. All he did know was that the sunlight moved slowly along the contour of the hill and, as the morning passed away, the light that had spilled down into the tunnel departed, and the shaft itself was once more steeped in its habitual gloom.

By now he had been joined by his sisters. They, too, were exceedingly hungry. None of them seemed able to do anything about it, and entirely ignored the remains of rabbits that littered the floor of the den. They wanted fresh meat such as their mother usually brought them. Moreover, they were thirsty but hesitated to leave the cairn to visit the depression where, as well they knew, there was water a-plenty.

At last the male took the initiative. He moved cautiously from under the pile of stones and stood upon the open hill. When he finally moved off to the depression and the watercourse, the others followed.

That action, slowly attempted, was their salvation. Just as they approached the depression, a long sinuous shape darted out from the thin scattering of rocks that crowned the hollow. An instant later, he had leaped onto the back of a buck rabbit nibbling at some moist grass. The stricken creature let out a shrill scream that startled the puppies who, in their sudden fear, crouched close together.

They witnessed the rabbit's sudden kick before he died, and then saw the stoat begin his gruesome feasting.

That was too much for the male pup. His hungry stomach rebelled. Losing all sense of caution, and knowing only that the slim, gray-coated creature was feasting on something his mother usually brought for both his and his sisters' enjoyment, he let out a sharp growl and hurled himself forward.

The stoat was badly startled, and leaping away from the

They moved down to the watercourse

rabbit he had slain, he beheld approaching the wild beast the puppy had so suddenly become. Behind him, urged on by his aggressive cries, came the rest of the excited family.

In a flash the stoat had swung about, and before any of the puppies could actually mark his departure from the scene of his recent conquest, he had vanished, leaving the rabbit to sustain their hungry stomachs.

While the sun went slanting down the sky, the puppies worried the carcass, eating and tearing at the flesh until little else but bones were left. When nothing more remained to attract them, they lay around in a circle waiting for the stoat to make another appearance and slay yet another rabbit as their mother had so often done.

Already they were more concerned with satisfying their voracious appetites than with listening and watching for the return of their parent. For them, she had been the means of providing for their comfort, and had the stoat continued to do so, they would have as easily accepted him as part of their intimate world, the loss of their mother passing almost unnoticed.

The stoat, however, having experienced a very sharp lesson, had departed to a less crowded part of the hill, and the puppies sat waiting in vain for another rabbit to be provided for their supper.

The sun went down beyond the horizon; the evening was cold and cheerless until there was a glow with the rising of yet another moon. Then, almost in despair, the puppies returned to the lair under the cairn, and the Hill of Hebron withdrew into the shadows until the moon should rise high in the sky and another lonely night began.

All five puppies slept restlessly that night. Some vague probing in the depths of their consciousness was telling them that the uniformity of their lives had come to an end. They sensed that the mother, who had hunted for them and attended to their every want, would never more return to the lair.

Time and time again they whined as they tried to sleep, curling themselves into tightly compressed balls of fur and no longer seeking to lie together. It was as though, aware that soon they must live independent of one another, instinctively they began to break the family bond that held them subject to collective action.

They were all up and about very early next morning, and because of the experience of the previous day, went to the water hole where they hoped to find another rabbit to satisfy their increasing hunger.

Nothing whatever did they see to intrigue and excite them. Even the few bits of fur from their earlier feasting had been scattered by the night wind.

Walking singly they went to the hollow where the water welled up from some hidden source, fresh and invigorating. They drank greedily as if hoping thus to ease the pangs of hunger.

It was another sunny day which, as the hours drew on toward high noon, grew stifling. Soon the puppies lay about the hollow, the stronger male alone remaining alert while his sisters slept.

A bird was croaking somewhere on the southern slopes. It was a raven, and suddenly he was answered by another of his tribe from the direction of the cairn. The young dog twitched his ears and then gave a heavy sigh. He knew it was useless to go to investigate. He was already growing wise, a wisdom suddenly thrust on him by the sheer necessity to live. This told him it would be futile to stalk a bird such as the black one, which even now was gazing at him from the summit of the cairn.

In that hour that was teaching the young animal so much, it seemed that the murmur of the spring water had increased in volume. The trickle that ran through the watercourse was now like the frail tinkle of a pipe such as any shepherd might hold to his lips to bring forth the comfort of sound in his solitude.

Although the puppy had no actual knowledge of either pipes or shepherds, some instinct handed down to him from his mother told him that these things existed.

Again he sighed, then found his attention directed to a clump of coarse grass that cast a heavy shadow on the westerly slope of the hill. First it was the movement of the grass itself that made him focus his eyes on the spot. Then it was the contrary breeze that completed the picture that was forming in his mind.

A rabbit was hidden behind that clump of grass!

The puppy raised himself, his ears pressed flat against his skull and his tail feathering after the manner of a mature shepherd dog about to round up sheep. His wet nose constantly tested the air.

One of the others awakened just then, but she, unlike her brother, was lazy, and much too miserable, to rouse herself sufficiently to determine what it was that held the young dog's attention.

It was just as well, for no doubt had she felt inclined to investigate what was attracting the other, they would have had no supper that evening. As it was, she rolled over on her side and went immediately into another sleep — this time more from weakness than anything else.

Meanwhile, the young dog, having accepted the fact that a rabbit was near by, and the picture now being fully formed in his mind, prepared to stalk the creature. Some rudimentary caution inherited from his mother came to his aid in the very instant he decided to act.

As he prepared to move forward, his body pressed low to the ground, he seemed to see his mother as last he had when she had been stalking game. Almost instinctively, he adopted the stance that had been her own characteristic stance. Perhaps in that moment of her puppies' necessity, something of her spirit returned to that depression on the Hill of Hebron to succor those who now had to learn to fend for themselves. Perhaps it was she who moved like a shadow before the young dog as he nosed his way silently toward that quivering clump of grass.

No sound came from him, despite his acute anxiety to catch and slay the unsuspecting rabbit. The wind also continued to aid him, blowing direct toward him and thus keeping his scent from the timid creature who was nibbling the close-cropped grass surrounding the coarse tussock that he fondly imagined was giving him protection.

Perhaps, amongst other things that late afternoon, the young dog's destiny was more strongly vested in his mother than in his own capabilities. Maybe it was she who possessed the very special virtue that made the rabbit sit up with its back turned to the enemy closing in on him.

Indeed, the creature had no actual knowledge of the identity of the animal that suddenly and silently pounced on it, and obtained a firm grip on the neck. Nor was it the grip that brought the rabbit so swiftly to death. It was sheer fright, the grip, after all, being too feeble to do much harm.

The moment the rabbit toppled onto its side, the puppy could no longer restrain himself. He let out a yell of excitement that brought his sisters stumbling to him.

All were soon engaged in the struggle to tear the rabbit into pieces. There were even sharp exchanges of anger amongst them as one succeeded in getting a larger share than the others.

Only when a raven flew low above them did the puppies cease their final tussle over the remains and think suddenly of their own safety.

That night, as if reminiscent of the rainy season, there was mist over the hill, and the now waning moon was like a wraith drifting through the sky. There was a chill wind, too, snaking over the rocks, and as the male puppy lay at the entrance of the lair guarding the sleep of the others, he sensed for the first time the inhospitality of the Hill of Hebron.

Afar off, he heard a faint grunt. Although he had no knowledge of the creature that had uttered such a sound, he did associate it with the alarm disclosed by his mother on those occasions when the noise had drifted to her from out of the night.

The puppy shivered as if with the touch of a dead paw upon his back and the thrust of a cold nose against his side.

Without understanding why, he turned about and went down into the lair where he continued to lie, unsleeping, listening and watching.

Out on the Hill of Hebron, the wild boars were again at their hunting!

4: The Shepherd from the Plains

IT CAME to pass that about this time, husbandmen were
searching for fresh tillage a little east of Gath, the village that
lay on the northern slopes of Hebron. Their normal sowing
time, extending from the tenth month onward, had been
satisfactorily accomplished, but the time had come for the
most ambitious amongst them to journey forth and attempt
a new tillage. Thus two of the younger men, setting out,
came close to the foothills of Hebron, and with them came a
shepherd, also seeking new territory.

Unlike the husbandmen, the shepherd was attracted to
the pastures that were reputed to lie along the entire coast-
line, extending up to the very foothills themselves. They
were watered, too, according to the tales told by nomads
coming out of Edom, by two rivers that rose up on the
heights of the southern hills about Beersheba.

The shepherd, Saul, last surviving son of Daniel the legendary herdsman of Arimathaea, had ever been anxious to
travel this new country beyond Gath, and hearing of the
husbandmen's intentions, he quickly gathered together
what few things he required and set forth with them.

It had been an easy journey. The weather had remained
for the most part fair, and the nights had been lit by the
moon which, on the third day of their travels, was at its

zenith. There had been much good pasture visible; good ground, too, for future tillage. Every night when the husbandmen and the shepherd sat around their campfire, they talked of nothing else but the good earth and the grassland.

It was agreed amongst them that when they returned to their own village, they would persuade their families to accompany them to this new place and there bide a while, to see what crops could be cultivated. The shepherd, as was natural in one who tended sheep and goats, thought not so much in terms of cultivation as he did of pasture. He knew, none the less, that the husbandmen with their crops would be necessary for his own survival in this strange land beneath the frown of the Hill of Hebron.

On the last of the full moon, while the husbandmen sought for a likely site for their families, the shepherd set out in an attempt to reach the neighborhood of the two rivers he had heard so much about from the wandering tribesmen from Edom. He considered it would be of advantage if he could find suitable grazing adjacent to one or other of the rivers, and a place in which he could set up his tent when the time came for him to live alone with his flock of sheep and his herd of goats.

Saul was no longer a young man; in fact, judging from his lined, bearded face, he was nigh to sixty years. Even so, due to his having always lived in the open air, he was yet lithe of limb when occasion demanded, and could bear himself upright. The manner of his measured tread was brought about not by age but by the slow movement of the thoughts in his head, rarely broken into by his companions on the hills, the sheep and the old dog who herded them.

Sheepherding had ever been a lonely occupation, and many a shepherd had become a philosopher as a result.

Thus on this day that was to see the last of the present phase of the moon, the shepherd plodded on steadily, flanking the foothills that straggled south to the Hill of Hebron. Here was most clearly marked the irregular mass of the main escarpment that was everywhere broken up into small ravines.

The shepherd noted that the grassland continued good save where the rocky ground thrust down into the plain in a series of undulating ledges and broken gullies.

When at last the noonday sun warned him that he should shelter a while and partake of some food, the shepherd retired into one of the ravines, and eating the goat meat he had brought with him, opened up the leather water carrier and drank deeply.

He was then well contented to lie in the shadows and ruminate upon the proposal put forward by the husbandmen. He liked this strange new country, with the hills breaking away to the south and the grassland so easily accessible. The ravines, similar to the one in which he now rested, would give ample protection against any sudden storm in the rainy season and, moreover, would certainly prove a boon to sheep distressed by the heat. Here, as he rested, the shepherd noted with satisfaction that it was cool, despite the noonday heat that shimmered beyond the protective bulk of the hills.

The old man must have dozed after a while, for he suddenly awakened with a start, the raucous cry of a raven disturbing him. As he opened his eyes and stared up at the very blue sky, he saw a bird swinging down in effortless flight and, marking it, saw it come to rest at a point high up the ravine.

Remembering that he had been anxious to locate the rivers that lay in the east, and discerning a suitable plateau a little below the place where the bird had rested, he decided to ascend the ravine, and from the plateau endeavor to determine the lay of the land eastward.

The old man gathered his few things together and started to climb. He walked very slowly, seeking to conserve himself for the more arduous ascent to the plateau itself when once he had reached the head of the ravine.

He had a feeling that he was saving himself a long journey, and that from the vantage point of the plateau, he would glimpse the fabled rivers and with them, perhaps, the land beyond Beersheba.

After an hour or so, the shepherd came to a narrow goat track winding up between high walls of limestone to the plateau, and following a short rest, prepared himself for the last part of the climb.

It was rough going. The trail became little more than a water gully about halfway up. The sun was swinging westward when Saul finally stood upon the wind-shapen ledge and stared due east.

As far as he could see stretched the uncompromising rock forks that broke away into ravines. No tree was visible in the whole of the panorama. Then as the rays of the sun drew level with the escarpment and streamed over the uplift of rock from west to east, the entire thrust of the mountain range became etched upon the eastern skyline.

The shepherd was then able to see the outward curve of the limestone hill upon which he stood, and noticed that it fell steeply toward what was clearly an amphitheater.

Shading his eyes the better to bridge the distance, Saul discerned what was now obviously a depression thrusting away from the main escarpment and following a northerly spur that shaped a watercourse.

The old man's eyes moved slowly over that distant landscape, and he uttered a scarcely perceptible sigh of satisfaction.

He nodded with understanding.

Without a doubt he was at last gazing upon the first of the twin rivers; and as he tried to trace out its course, the gleam of silver striking up sharply enabled him finally to follow the northward run toward the sea.

Not long afterward, as the sun traveled lower down the sky, and the almost transparent afternoon revealed the more remote horizons, Saul saw with startling clearness the greater river in the northeast. Between it and the first lay the greenest of green country, the best, the old shepherd felt, in the whole land of Edom and Judaea.

He decided then and there that when another week had come and gone, and he had returned again to his home village, he would rest but a few days. Then he would saddle an ass and come once more to this land: and, with none then to dispute his journeying, travel to that country of the two rivers, and maybe seek out the high hills and discover what lay on them.

A short while later found Saul on his way down the ravine, but it was long after the full moon had burst above the mountains that he came at last to the camp where the husbandmen were showing concern over his long absence.

In reply to their eager questioning, he gave but little information, merely saying that he had found the rivers he sought, and with them, the grazing he required for his sheep and goats.

The others, knowing full well his morose nature, pressed him no further when they found him slow in speech. Since next day they planned to return to their home village, they retired within the hour and slept soundly, thus repairing their strength for the long journey they had to make when the morning was young.

After the departure of the husbandmen and the shepherd to their native village, the moon fast waned until soon there was no moon at all, only the starlight. Though the sky was growing less dark night by night the time drew near for the early harvest of the plains, which started in the third month and lasted until well into the sixth.

On the barren Mount of Hebron, the puppies found it difficult to live. None as yet was adequately equipped to survive without a more experienced animal to hunt for them — none save perhaps the male puppy.

Other animals that dwelt on the hill were well aware of the puppies' inexperience in the almost instinctive matter of hunting. Because they were wise with the inherent wisdom of the wild, they took advantage by cropping the grass within a dozen feet or so of the young ones' noses.

Only when the male pup himself was much in evidence did these other small creatures show more caution. Fortunately for him there were times when one less alert than his fellows would fall a victim to the pup's sudden attack.

Such spasmodic feeding could not keep the family from starvation. Indeed, their inability to fend for themselves would have become apparent much sooner had not the male found a way to the ravens' nesting site and constantly robbed it.

As it was, the food they obtained in this way only brought the wrath of the entire raven clan upon them. An old bird, returning unexpectedly from a foraging expedition, surprised the raider and drove him off. Not long afterward, a flock of ravens made an appearance over the hill, led by the ancient one who had essayed an assault on the pup.

They settled on the nesting site and filled the air with their raucous cries. Then it seemed they were holding counsel together, cawking one to the other and blinking, while in an abstracted way keeping the puppies within their line of vision, who, as was now their habit, were dozing restlessly in the hollow near the run of water.

At the same time, an advance guard had been set on a high rock adjacent to the watercourse — a raven large and sleek that sat silent and unmoving like some black creature of vengeance.

The male pup had a queer feeling that the sentinel was watching him. Retaining only too vividly the memory of the unexpected encounter with the very old bird on the lime-whitened rocks where the entire colony nested, he sensed that the gathering of the dark-feathered clan had something to do with his frequent visits to the nests.

For over an hour the conference went on, the birds caw-

cawking, and the silent guard taking no part in the proceed-
ings, but merely sitting motionless on his vantage point,
watching.

Then, without warning, the attack came.

The air suddenly darkened, and a score or more ravens
dove down upon the hollow and the now terror-stricken puppies. The birds made no encircling maneuver prior to the
attack, but went straight into action, the solitary sentinel also
joining in by diving down upon the male.

Due to his watchfulness, he was not taken so completely
by surprise as were his sisters. As the huge bird dropped
down upon him, with beak poised and talons extended, he
rolled out of the way, and before the bird could recover from
the stoop he made, the puppy was on him, a creature of the
utmost savagery. He snapped and lunged at the raven, and
succeeded in disabling one wing. This made the end more
sure for the young dog, with the bird fluttering helplessly,
he leaped on its back, and bit through the neck feathers.

His jaws held, despite the raven's frenzied attempts to
break free, and in a few moments, accompanied by an ago-
nizing croak, the bird's neck was broken and he died just as
the rest of the ravens succeeded in slaying two of the female
puppies and driving the others in terror to the security of the
lair.

The assault had taken less than two minutes, yet in that
short space of time the pups' familiar world was destroyed
and such security as they had till then enjoyed was shattered
forever.

Together with the male who was sore after the terrible
buffeting he, too, had received, they crouched deep in the

lair — a sadly depleted family whose days were surely numbered.

Outside, another night came down over the scene of the conflict. It was a very silent night, too. No night bird called now. The common bond that united all who inhabited the wild had been rudely severed. Even if the wild boars — the most hated of all creatures — were at the entrance of the lair under the cairn, no bird now would warn the puppies.

The bond of the feathered tribe — one for the other — was a bond as enduring as time itself; and the pups, having offended the tribe, could never more depend on the usual warnings of danger that only birds can give.

From henceforth only the wind could succor and aid them in their tenacious hold on life. Like their mother, they had become outcasts, and as outcasts in the world of the wild, they would become easy victims to those other creatures banded together in an effort to survive.

In due course, the harvesttime of the plains would see the garnering of those whose advent into an alien world had been but an incident in the centuries the Hill of Hebron had known.

Only one of the puppies would leave the hill alive!

5: The Last Flowering of the Old Fig Tree

NORTHEAST of the Hill of Hebron, and not a great distance from the rising of the western fork of the river near Beersheba, was a very ancient fig tree, withered and nigh dead, and yet still clinging tenaciously to life. It cast little shade upon the broken ground that gave it such scant roothold. When the sun threw its shadow it was little more than the outline of a broken gibbet, crooked and ugly. No bird nested in it, not even a wandering bird of prey came near. In its slow dying, the old fig tree was the most despised of anything that grew in a place where growing was a struggle that twisted and bent the strongest.

Yet its day of death was still far distant, for to it came one lonely creature, seeing in it something less cruel than the summit of the hill where a cave beneath a cairn no longer offered protection. An enemy, greater than the ravens, had suddenly taken an exceptional interest in it, drawn first by the hollow where water rose from a hidden source and fell in a glittering stream down a timeworn gully where lay two pathetic bits of fur and bone.

The young male dog, last of the litter of the shepherd bitch, had spent a night of terror in the lair while a boar of formidable size grunted and scratched at the cairn of stones. The stench was an abomination, but the young dog, terrified almost into a state of paralysis, bore it rather than venture up into the outer tunnel. He could hear the boar's grunts of anger, and at times there was a slow trickling of earth into the lair as the creature above renewed his attack on the stones.

While he had known many other nights that seemed endless, and when danger had seemed imminent, none had been so prolonged as this.

He was, moreover, thin and weak. During the past few days that weakness had so increased that he had difficulty in moving with any show of his old vigor. He had scarcely noticed the departure of his two remaining sisters from the lair, never more to return. Each had the previous day presented an easy prey for the ravens. They had died close to the hollow where, in their distress, they had gone for water. Now the young dog lay quivering all alone.

At last, the long night drew to its end, and as the dawn came up, a crimson dawn, with color in the east spilling out over the sky like the wild spreading of blood, the boar grew weary of his efforts to gain entrance to the lair. He finally went off at a slow trot, grumbling with each step he took, and not stopping to drink again from the hollow which had attracted him because of what he had twice found there — fur and bones not quite picked clean by the ravens.

There was little to make the young dog wish to remain in this place where he had been born. His memories of the cave, even of the hill itself, were tinged with the events of the last few days. Starvation, and constant fear, had taken from him the resourcefulness that had, until recently, sustained him.

It was, however, a very long time before he felt the insistent urge to venture forth. During the long night it seemed that he had acquired the mature knowledge of an animal more than twice his age. Danger had sharpened his perceptions; his sense of smell told him much, and he knew exactly what was going on outside the lair. He had long been aware that the boar that had threatened his existence had departed before he made a motion.

Eventually, the young animal started to move very quietly up the narrow tunnel until he crouched in the hollow under the cairn. Through the small crevasse that opened out onto the hill itself, he could see the sunlight quivering. For a while longer, he remained safe under the pile of stones. In his mind lurked the growing conviction that if he were to continue living, he would have to go forth and seek out other living creatures that, if slain, would sustain him. Up to now hunting had been more or less accidental, requiring the presence of prey to put him into action.

He had become aware, without the slightest element of doubt, that as he had hunted down small creatures in the past, he would have to do so in the future with even greater ardor, despite the weakness he now felt due to hunger.

The dog wriggled as he lay quietly looking out onto the hill. He knew that he was quite alone, that his sisters were dead, and this in spite of the fact that he possessed no real knowledge of death.

Thirst made him finally creep out. Standing with tail tucked under his legs, he tested the atmosphere, and found nothing in it to cause him apprehension. Even the ravens appeared to be far away on other more important business.

The animal's confidence grew; his stance took on firmer lines, and his tail feathered a little. He went finally to the hollow and the stream, and drinking his fill at a point where the water was running clear and fast, he moved off in a northeasterly direction, striking what appeared to be an ill-defined track.

Perhaps his departure from the hill at such an opportune hour was not completely overlooked by the Spirit of Fur and Hide, for the dog had not been long on his way when a flash of yellow on the trail ahead brought to him an awareness of some other creature in the vicinity besides himself. He then discerned something else — the gray-furred shape of a creature brought low by that other one that had made so hasty a retreat.

The young dog let out a yelp of delight. What had happened before — way up on the Hill of Hebron — had happened again. A weasel-like creature had made a kill, leaving it because of fear for another to consume.

He was soon at his feasting, and since he was so hungry just ate the slain animal where it lay on the trail. Not long afterward, he moved to a shady spot between two boulders and rested with his head pillowed on his outstretched paws. Life was suddenly taking on a new and vigorous meaning. Because he no longer had the other puppies to consider, and could move more freely away from the dangers of the summit of the hill, his fears departed, and a new confidence sprang up in him.

Moreover, as the meal he had eaten strengthened him,

and quickened the flowing of blood through his veins, so did he relax. When he prepared to move off once more, he did so with an easy swing of his body, his eyes keenly alert, and his tail half raised.

Then for a second time that day did the Spirit of Fur and Hide take special care of him. Another small creature crossed his path. The dog leaped forward without a sound, and as his jaws closed on the gray neck, death came to the hapless rodent with a suddenness that was no more than the sharp falling of darkness on a hillside that but an instant before had been red with the glow of the sunset.

That night, the dog crept between the uprising walls of a gully for shelter. Finding a spot that suited the curl of his body in repose, he slept more peacefully than he had done for many a night past. There was, unknown to him, constant movement on the hill — night birds passing over — other, more grim, hunters moving up over the northerly contours. None, however, came near the gully where the young dog slept. The wind, blowing from west to east, did not carry his scent to any who sought his kind for prey, and when the dawn came, the wind had run its course, and there was no danger whatever for one such as he.

The young dog awakened, stretched himself and yawned. Then leaving the gully he continued on his trek downhill, no longer aware of weakness, but only of an increasing strength.

On that second day of his journeying, the dog had come to the encircling loop in the range of mountains that protected the spring which was the source of the first of the two rivers near which was the village of Beersheba. Not long afterward, as the sun went down and the evening star glimmered like a lamp lit and shining bright, the wandering dog approached the old fig tree that more than ever possessed the appearance of a broken gibbet, crooked and ugly.

Once again, as on the previous night, he slept in complete peace.

The Spirit of Fur and Hide continued to keep him safe as, down in the green plain beside the river, a shepherd kept safe the sheep he had brought hence from the distant village of Gath that lay below the northern slopes of the ancient Hill of Hebron.

The ungodly, reasoning amongst themselves, but not with any display of wisdom, have often said that life is short and tedious, and in the fullness of time there is no remedy for the decay of the things of the earth. Breath in the living creature is as the smoke of the nostrils, and the beating of the heart no more than a little spark. Man, and all living things, are born of adventure, and in the end are nothing!

Nothing indeed had been the old fig tree until the young dog came to rest beneath it, finding amongst the ancient roots a hollow, safe and warm, which brought him back to it night after night. Perhaps because a living creature, warm and waxing strong in knowledge day after day, had come to make a home beneath its withered trunk and to scratch amidst its dry roots, a new surging of sap began to bring back a sheen to the ancient branches that, in the hour of dawn and sunset, cast a shadow upon the ground that was awesome and seemed to bear witness to the end of all malefactors.

The man stretched out his hand

The dog sensed that on this part of the mountain, close to a green plain where hunting was most profitable, there was no danger for him. Thus he tarried until a week became a month, and the month waned to bring in another week and another month.

More than ever did he sense that this was a good place in which to dwell, for in all that time none threatened his existence under the old fig tree. No matter how far he wandered out into the plain, he never failed to return to the hill beyond the western fork of the river, and to that gibbet-like shape that stood up so crooked and ugly in the flare of the sunset.

Though time itself is little more than a shadow that so soon passes away, there is always the returning light of another day not far off; and it was in the dawn of a new day that Saul came up the mountain, attracted by the shape of the old fig tree, naked on the hillside in the golden glory of the sunrise.

The lonely-living man thus came upon the lonely-living dog. The dog, never having seen before one like the old shepherd, stared up in wonder, and the man dropped onto one knee with hand outstretched. In the amber spilling of the sunrise, there was something in his manner that made the dog turn to him.

So to the shepherd of the plain came the dog no one had wanted, and upon him fell the destiny which his mother had so violently rejected to give him birth.

6: The Beginning of Bondage

OF THOSE who had made up his family in the lair on the Hill of Hebron, the nameless dog, now suddenly allied to man, the Great Master, was the one that most closely resembled his mother. His head was surely that of a pure sheepherding dog, and his general coloring, similar to that of most domestic animals in or about the villages of the plain, gave no clue to the wild dog who had been his sire.

While the young dog was not given to direct thinking as understood by man, he yet had his own ways of arriving at certain conclusions. In the short time he had lived, dependence on his natural instincts to survive had enabled him to overcome the many terrors of the Hill of Hebron.

Those same instincts were hard at work when he beheld the shepherd kneeling before him, holding out one hand and talking to him in sounds he could not understand. Yet, because his mother had been an animal in close contact with man, they somehow found a dim response in his brain.

Even so, there was something else in him — a primitive hatred of man inherited from his father, the wild dog. This held him apprehensive and motionless while every nerve in his body quivered.

The shepherd could see the fear deep in the young dog's

eyes, and was moved to pity. He could see also that the animal had had little or no contact with man, and could only conclude that he had been born in the wild, possibly the offspring of some wayward one who had deserted her master to rear her young. Saul searched amidst his raiment, bringing forth a long coil of hemp.

The dog watched him anxiously. His hind legs twitched as if he contemplated making a sudden escape.

Before he could stir himself into action, the hand of the shepherd descended upon him, and he felt for the first time the encircling loop of hemp about his neck. As it tightened, he knew instinctively that he belonged to the strange being who bent over him. It was not just a matter of the hemp coil.

He cowered down and snarled at his captor. The next instant he felt a sharp tug at his neck. Even while he endeavored to dig in with his hind legs, he felt himself hauled from the hollow he had made amidst the roots of the fig tree, where, for a brief period, he had been so contented. Was he never to know content for long?

Despite his struggling, the shepherd got him down off the hill, and by high noon the dog was tethered to a stake driven deep into the ground.

Now began the long days of servitude, the days of learning, the days of trouble and anxiety. The young dog from the wilds of Hebron was not altogether a willing pupil, having been born free. He found it difficult to accept a master, and could not understand why he was kept constantly at the end of a tether. Why, instead of hunting down his own food, was it now given to him by the man, who visited him frequently throughout the day? The dog was in a continual state of fear, accentuated when the shepherd's old dog decided to investigate him at close quarters. He was of a friendly disposition.

He had grown old in the service of his master, and was tolerant of anything the shepherd took under his care. Moreover, the dog was all too keenly aware that the herding of sheep was more taxing for him than it used to be. Reasoning after the manner of his kind, he was already sensing that perhaps the young animal was to undergo some sort of instruction in the work with ewes and lambs, and, in due time, relieve him a little of his responsibilities.

After the first few days, the younger animal began to feel less fearful when he came on one of his visits of inspection. What gave the young dog greater confidence was the fact that the sheep dog made no attempt to take from him the meat the man brought at midday. Remembering the many squabbles between his sisters over scraps of food that had been left unattended for a short while, he could not help regarding this as a favorable sign of the other animal's acceptance of him.

Even so, there was still the sense of fear because of the tether that limited his freedom. He felt that he was at a disadvantage before any enemies, furred or feathered. He still remembered vividly the attacks the ravens had made on him and his sisters.

After five days at the end of the tether, something else upsetting happened to him. The shepherd approached one evening and slipped a collar of hide about his neck. Following this, the man put another strip of hide through it and then tried to coax the now thoroughly disconcerted dog to follow him. The old sheep dog stood at a respectful distance watching.

Again and yet again did the shepherd tug at the offending collar, and again and yet again did the captive animal resist. To be on the end of a similar tether that merely kept him within a certain ranging distance of the stake was certainly preferable. The man had already done much the same thing when he brought him down off the hill and the dog did not care for it.

The more the shepherd pulled, the more the dog tugged against him. In the end, the animal commenced to wail in his utter distress and fear. The shepherd, realizing that he would have to act with greater understanding if he were to obtain the dog's trust, retired to think of some other plan.

To say the least, Saul was disconcerted. Having spent so many years of his active life with sheepherding animals responsive to his every command, he did not know how to combat the young dog's distrust. All those animals he had known in the past, without exception, had been dogs closely associated with man and his way of life. His old dog had been sired by a sheepherding dog of some consequence, dwelling not far from his home. At a very early age, this one had shown a marked interest in sheep, and was not long in mastering the first lessons in herding. Saul could not remember having had a dog that was more easily trained.

Next evening, Saul was still pondering the problem when he noticed, as the evening shadows closed in, the young dog had made a definite attempt to move in toward the campfire. The old dog had taken up a position close by, and after a short while both were resting their heads on outstretched paws, staring at the flickering of the fire over which, scarcely half an hour before, Saul had prepared his evening meal.

An idea then took shape in the shepherd's mind. He turned his head to regard with particular interest the attitudes of the two dogs.

He then rose quietly to his feet and moved slowly toward the animals. Bending down, he patted the head of the old dog before moving on to the other. He then slid a strip of hide into the young dog's collar while speaking to him soothingly, and at the same time releasing him from the main tether.

Still speaking gently to the unsuspecting animal, he started to retrace his steps in the direction of the fire, letting the hide leash pass through his fingers. A quietly uttered word to the old dog brought the animal to his feet to follow him. A few seconds later both were sitting down before the fire, the shepherd retaining his hold on the leash which was now fully extended. He then proceeded to draw it in a little, perceptibly tugging at the young dog's collar.

There was nothing hasty in his tugging; in fact, it was scarcely felt at first, so lightly was it done. Then the tug on the collar was a trifle more compelling, and the young dog, conscious of it, started to move in until, without being actually aware of what was happening, he, too, lay within reach of the heat of the fire.

Saul nodded his head with satisfaction. So much had been accomplished by such a simple act. Still keeping a firm hold on the leash, he ceased studying the dog's reactions and gazed into the heart of the fire.

He was thinking that by such subtle manipulation, coupled with a softly spoken word or two, he might well gain the animal's complete trust, and with that firmly established he could then proceed to other more important things.

Once again Saul nodded his head. He heard, seemingly from a long way off, the howling of some jackals. The shadows deepened, until beyond the ring of light cast by the fire, there was only the darkness.

At last the shepherd discerned that the young dog had moved in even closer and was now lying less than a foot from his cooking pots. He sniffed them with a familiarity that seemed to show he recognized that the food he sometimes had was heated in them.

Not long afterward the dog was asleep, no longer afraid, but quite clearly at ease, the heat from the fire being both comforting and reassuring.

What Saul did not know was that before approaching so close to the fire, the dog had been testing the wood smoke. For the past few days he had been familiar with it. There was something in the scent that attracted him. Somewhere in his consciousness lurked the age-old knowledge that had been his mother's, she who had known man and had often slept before campfires such as this one that burned so brightly.

When he did eventually start to move in, crawling low to the ground, his eyes never left the figure of the shepherd. So long as Saul made no move in his direction he experienced no misgiving, not even when there came some chance tug on the hide collar which he detested so heartily. Then for some minutes the dog lay just within the ring of firelight, sniffing the scent of the wood smoke and once again sensing that curious familiarity.

He was also fully aware of the nearness of the old dog, and was greatly comforted by the knowledge. Since the other animal possessed no fear of that flickering heat that seemed to drive the night shadows so far off, the young dog was also unaware of fear.

It was therefore a perfectly natural thing for him to move in closer until he lay within reach of the cooking pots with their tantalizing odor of boiled meat and herbs.

Following this daring move on his part, the moments seemed almost as long as that terrible night he had spent alone in the lair while the boar outside had sniffed and scratched for entrance.

There was, however, in this eternity of nervous anticipation, none of the apprehension of that night. The young dog was only overanxious lest the man-god suddenly disapprove of his action, and send him back to that outer darkness where the distant howling of jackals seemed louder and, as a result, more terrifying to one such as he.

Then, because there was no sign from the man, the young dog became so emboldened as to sniff the pots, aware all the time of an increasing sense of restfulness and a curious desire for complete relaxation as in the attitude of the old dog.

Not long after that, the young dog yielded to his happy impulses and lay asleep with his head on his paws. And in that sleep of contentment he whined, not because of troublesome dreams of the past, but because he was at last where all dogs should be who had suddenly become the companions of man!

7: No More To Go Hungry

SAUL'S CAMPING site in the valley of the two rivers had been well chosen. The grass thereabouts was greener than that under the cliffs of the escarpment, and a growth of rough scrub gave him all the fuel he needed for his nightly fire. More than that, a group of olive trees, long past their prime and as nigh faded as the old fig tree, grew within a couple of hundred yards or so of the camp. During the noonday heat the old shepherd sometimes went there to take his ease, and soon, out of consideration for the young dog, brought him to the place also in order that he, too, could take shelter from the heat and suffer no harm.

The animal sensed that Saul meant only to do well by him, and from the very hour when the shepherd brought him under the shade of the olives, there came a change in the dog's nature that had already been softened by his evening encounters with the comfort of Saul's fire. His was a complete lack of fear when Saul handled him, and he was no longer apprehensive of the collar and the hide strip that was sometimes put into it so that Saul could take him from one place to another.

Saul was quick to notice the change in the dog, the first sign being that the animal no longer snarled when either he or the old dog approached him.

Thus, by being patient, and continually speaking to him, Saul overcame the young dog's instinctive reactions to being in captivity. There eventually came a day when the animal, reluctantly it was true, permitted himself to be led far down into the plain and taken amongst the sheep.

This was an exciting experience. There were many young lambs, and all tumbled away as he was led amongst them. Although there were moments when he felt the desire to scatter them, he refrained, sensing that it would meet with Saul's complete disapproval. One other factor held him in restraint, and that was the old dog's attitude; he noted with increasing wonder how the older dog moved with gentleness amongst ewes and lambs alike, and none showed fear of him. He noted, too, that whenever one or two strayed from the main flock, without instruction from his master, the old dog trotted off, and after encircling the offenders drove them back into the fold.

Oddly enough, the young dog had a feeling of having been a witness to all this before. It was his mother's blood that remembered, telling him that to care for and protect sheep was the task of most dogs born in the villages of man and taken up in the hills and the pastures. It was a dog's heritage to work, and become the helpmate of man!

These were the days when Saul was constantly busy, and such moments as he could give to the young dog's training were less effective than he had hoped. Time was necessary to foster complete understanding and obedience in the animal. Even so, the dog was expressing pleasure whenever Saul came near him, and it was apparent that a bond was springing up between them.

Then on an evening that was cool and clear, Saul decided to go a little way up into the hills. He took with him the old dog, leaving the younger animal tethered under the olives.

The young dog sat on his haunches, watching the two depart, with a certain wistfulness in his eyes. He did not like being left behind, and would have been glad to have accompanied them even if it had meant following at the end of the tether.

For a long time he sat waiting and watching, often moving from one posture to another, and finally standing with head alert and eyes staring away into the hollows where the evening was fast setting up its tents. He shifted from one foot to another, anxious and wondering. . . .

Then he beheld Saul and the old dog come down off the narrow trail, and he could not contain himself, but let out a great howl that went echoing out across the plain.

Saul heard him and smiled. In that howl, he heard a note that had not been in the animal's voice before, a note of welcome. Maybe, on the morrow, he would go once again into the hills, journeying perhaps as far as the old fig tree, taking the young dog with him. Thus, as in the case of himself and the old dog, would he endeavor to strengthen the bond of their companionship.

The shepherd sat for a long time that night before the fire, with the old dog and the young one close beside him. The night drew its cloak fast about the camp, and when the stars came out, large and bright, a little wind came, too, and sang a melancholy song in the olives — a song as old as time itself.

At last, all three — the shepherd and the two dogs — slept

to its frail accompaniment, and the fire died in its ashes until only a dull red glow remained to tell of the life it had possessed when the night was young.

Next day was the Sabbath, and Saul tried out a daring experiment. He let the young dog run free. At first the animal seemed entirely unaware that he could move where he wished. When he did he was hungry and came readily to Saul's bidding to eat the meat he had prepared.

Ever since he was a young man, Saul had set part of the Sabbath aside for meditation. After a light repast, he retired to the shade of the olives, having first put the impressionable dog once again on a tether.

After a while the shepherd dozed, and with his bearded chin sunk deep on his chest, he dreamed that the grove of olives was the same grove where, as a lad, he used to play with his brothers. No movement came from him as he dreamed. He might well have been a man newly dead. At his feet, a pool of sunshine gathered slowly, and the young dog's gaze became concentrated on it.

He ignored the many small runways between the trees where shafts of sunlight, falling in pale splashes of indefinite color, reflected the leaf patterns. It was that single pool of sunlight that attracted him so much. At last he could not resist creeping toward it until he lay within its magic glow, his nose close to the old man's sandaled feet.

When Saul awakened and looked down, he was both elated and surprised, suddenly realizing that of his own free will the dog had come to him.

That evening he kept the promise he had made to himself the previous night. He went up into the hills, taking the young dog with him. It was another night of slow-fading light with a new moon sinking in the west. Then just as the last of the stars came out, Saul brought the dog to the old fig tree and paused a while to see what effect the visit might have on him.

The dog scratched at the roots, sniffing around eagerly. He recognized this as the wallow where he had lain content and happy after his journey from the Hill of Hebron. Even so, the very instant Saul set off down the trail that led to the camp, he had no need to tug at the tether. The dog followed willingly enough. In the gloom, the shepherd could see the animal's eyes shining as they gazed up into his face.

Saul smiled. He sensed that the animal was waving his tail with every step he took. The shepherd felt satisfied. He had not been overoptimistic after all in thinking that the dog had accepted him as his master. If greater proof were needed, what more could he wish than this — an expression of the animal's complete joy in following him after visiting the place in which he had previously made his lair?

Back up the hill, the crooked shape of the fig tree seemed less harsh in outline. A crown of stars seemed caught in the twisted branches. Then, within a few minutes of Saul and the dog departing for the plain, a night bird came winging in from the east, and took lodging in the branches — the first bird to settle on the tree for many a long year.

The bird was still there when the dawn flamed, and by noon he had started to build a nest.

When evening came again, it seemed that another tree stood up on that barren stretch of hillside. The gibbet-like appearance had somehow been taken away.

The dog felt the huge stone quiver

That same week following that memorable Sabbath, Saul took the young dog with him whenever he went out to attend to the sheep. The old dog, knowing the training of the inexperienced animal would soon begin in earnest, was never far off when the shepherd went amongst the flock.

Yet the young dog's first experience came not with the sheep but with some of the goats that were obstinate and persistent roamers. Saul had them tethered near a stretch of rough scrubland, but two had managed to slip their halters and wandered up amongst the rocks from which it would be difficult to dislodge them.

He decided to let the young dog run free, and see if he could not be of some assistance in bringing the goats down from their lofty refuge.

Saul uttered, without thinking, the word he normally used in sending the old dog off to round up wayward beasts. He little expected the young animal's response. To his surprise, the dog, following the direction he had indicated, was away so quickly that the shepherd gave a startled gasp. Two or three minutes later, the animal was up amongst the scattering of rocks and quite clearly prepared to tackle the goats without further ado.

He stood on a boulder, looking down at the two highly suspicious creatures. He then gave a short bark and took up a stance that left no doubt in the minds of the goats as to his general intention.

This, however, was more than they were willing to accept from a strange dog. Being old and wise, they made a concerted attack on the boulder, and the dog felt the huge stone quiver beneath his feet.

He was, nonetheless, fully determined to withstand any assault made against him. His body stiffened, and his feet splayed a little in order to keep a firm hold on the rock. Thus, when a second attempt was made to dislodge him from the boulder, he was fully prepared and acted suddenly. He leaped down, and before the goats could recover from the violent attempt they had made to move the rock, the dog was hard at their heels, and both creatures fled, making with all speed for the herd and their gesticulating master.

Saul was pleased the dog had suffered no harm, and knew that it would be only a matter of time before he could exact his complete obedience. Moreover he felt that the dog possessed the instinctive reactions of a pure sheepherding animal.

Saul kept the young dog at his side, and with great patience taught him how to keep sheep from straying. The only real fault he could find in him was one of nervous excitement whenever the sheep showed signs of scattering. In a month or so, however, the shepherd felt positive the dog would be as good as the old fellow whose limbs were fast becoming stiff with age.

Time, Saul considered, dealt with both young and old alike. To the former it brought experience and a joy in living; to the latter it wrought a weariness of the body and a desire for rest.

It was the ruthless hourglass of bloom and decay!

8: The Instincts of the Wild

ALTHOUGH SAUL had never given the young dog a name, the animal knew whenever the shepherd called him that it was he who should obey and not the old dog. Moreover, it was not long before he knew from the tone of his master's voice whether a command was being uttered, or just a casual remark. Saul, because of his lonely existence, often carried on a conversation with the dogs, and sometimes spoke to one or two of the ewes who seemed specially favored.

Despite his uncertain upbringing on the Hill of Hebron, and the inherent wildness in his nature, the young dog was quite happy in his new-found life with Saul. There was a certain security about it that soon subdued his natural fears, and it was only now and again that he harkened to the warm surging of the blood in his veins and felt a curious yearning to run free under the stars.

In such moments he would raise his head and listen, and the old scents and sounds would seem to come back to him, and he would see once again the barren heights of the Hill of Hebron, and hear the anxious whining of his sisters and the distant honking of the ravens.

Once, in such a moment of remembering, he saw his mother, her head half-tilted as she looked down at him, and her eyes shining with a strange sort of happiness as if she knew that at last her erring offspring was safe and was to do his duty toward man in an effort to atone for her many short-comings.

It seemed that his singing blood possessed the power to bring so much alive, even shapes from out of a past that had its being long before he was born.

It was always when there was a moon high in the sky that his blood sang the loudest, and obscure impulses caused his limbs to twitch and he whined softly.

Maybe the old dog was aware of the things that ofttimes troubled his companion, for he was seldom at ease on those nights when the young dog whined and his limbs twitched. Perhaps he, too, saw those shapes the other glimpsed — saw them and understood how dangerous they might be to fol-low in the gloom of the hills when the moonlight enticed the inhabitants of the wild to hunt and play.

The old dog, however, was not there when his com-panion finally obeyed the call in his blood.

It was a night similar to that when his mother set off from the lair on her last hunting expedition. The full moon was soaring up over the hills, and out on the plain some jackals were howling as they hunted. Due to the close approach of the jackals, Saul and the old dog had gone to ensure the flock's being safe. The young animal, left by the campfire, lay dozing peacefully until the warm surging of his blood suddenly brought him to his feet. It was then he realized the tether that held him captive was loose about his neck, and it was an instinctive act on his part to lower his head and step free.

As the strip of hide fell from him he merely quivered, but

did not move. His head, notwithstanding, was turned in the direction of the hills, and as he adopted the stance of his kind, his body, in the firelight, appeared slender and rangy, and his attitude more that of a wolf than of a dog. His wild father in him was to the fore.

Then he started to move off, heading noiselessly for the dark line of cliffs that marked the approaches to the main escarpment. At first he moved cautiously, finally breaking into a steady lope. Soon he was heading up the trail that led to the old fig tree and the solitary stretches of mountain that cumulated in the Hill of Hebron itself.

The young dog knew no fear on this night of his journey back to the wild solitudes. He only knew that he was running as he had never run before, his limbs taking him with ease over the rough stones. He had no regard for what the night might bring.

He came upon the fig tree quite suddenly, little realizing that he had traveled so far up the hill. He saw it, queerly transfixed against the burnished shield of the moon which lay far back on a purple sky.

The dog paused for a few seconds, staring upward. He knew it was his own special tree that he glimpsed, but somehow it seemed different. He investigated the roots. Even when he pressed on up the slope, he was still uncertain, and twice paused to glance back. Moving up into the diaphanous moonglow, he could not see the shape of the tree very clearly, and after a third glance back along the trail, he forgot it entirely.

An hour later he had hit the broken track much used by

the marauding jackals, and saw it running on and on like a twisting thread in the moonlight.

When he paused to gain his breath, he thought he heard a voice calling from far down the hillside. He pricked his ears to listen more intently. For a while he stood gazing back along the trail; but all he could hear was the murmur of the breeze bidding him follow. There was nothing else.

Then he obeyed the call, and set his head toward the heights of Hebron.

The dog continued to thrust on up the broken slope, unwittingly keeping to the trail so recently taken by a pack of jackals — part of the main body that had gone questing in the plain and caused Saul so much apprehension.

In the golden light of the full moon, every object was sharply revealed, and the dog's eyes were constantly adjusting to both near and distant outlines, and at the same time becoming more and more accustomed to the alternating shades of brightness. Suddenly he saw rising up ahead a broken ravine that was filled with debris of unaccountable age. He somehow misjudged the distance that separated him from it, for first it appeared to be very remote, then within a pace or two of his fast-moving feet.

He pulled up abruptly, and noticed that the opposite wall of the ravine was an uprising cliff that towered high out of the gloom below until it was nothing but a serrated shape against the moonlit sky that outtowered even the mountain.

The dog was fast approaching the area of Mount Hebron much frequented by the jackals and within a few miles of the fateful hollow where his mother had lost her life. He continued along the edge of the ravine until he came to a scattering of debris that made it possible for him to pick his way cautiously across to the other side. Thus, by following a natural cleavage in the escarpment, crossed by way of a natural bridge of rubble, he did what creatures of the wild had done from time immemorial, and stood at last in the hunting territory of the jackals.

Then, for the first time that night, a great fear came upon him. He looked back over his shoulder at the awesome crevasse he had crossed. This was a world both hostile and unknown. His lips wrinkled as the fear in him demanded some outward acknowledgment. The hair stood stiffly on his back and neck, his tail dropped between his legs.

He felt lost and helpless. Something seemed to have reached out from the magic of the night and challenged him to fight it and survive.

The snarl on his lips grew, then he ceased to snarl and only strained his ears to listen. Rising up from out of the mountain wastes came a call he recognized—the call of his own kind.

The wild dogs, or jackals, were on the meat trail!

No longer was he conscious of fear; he seemed to grow in stature. A second later, he was loping off to where the distant hunting call rose and fell, and all the yellow brothers of the wild were gathering to follow a leader and hunt down that which, under somewhat different circumstances, they would have feared.

With the wild, there was always safety and courage in numbers.

For a long time, the young dog ran along the track that

hugged the crevasse; then the trail opened out until he found himself running full into the moonlight and following what was clearly the warm scent of the pack.

No sound did he hear now. The jackals were obviously running mute as if close on the heels of the creature that, by sheer force of numbers, they sought to bring down.

The dreadful attack had already been shaped when the young dog came upon a hollow surrounded with hummocks. All he saw was an old boar held at bay by some fifteen wild dogs, not one of whom seemed willing to leap for the fateful throat hold.

Strange as the scene appeared to be, the newcomer recognized it from out of that shadowland of the past evoked by his singing blood. Unheeded by the others who were arranged in a semicircle around the boar, he crept forward. A place was made for him in the grim throng, and he was standing beside another like himself. His companion had not even given him a glance, but had kept his eyes fixed steadfastly on the tusked creature before him.

Once again the hair on the young dog's back and neck stiffened. But this time it was not from fear, but from the primitive desire to help slay one both lawful prey and ancient enemy.

Not a sound came from the encircling jackals; not a sound from their intended victim. Then, imperceptibly, the dread semicircle closed in a little. The boar grunted in anger, his eyes gleaming.

Smaller became the semicircle until it was a half circle no longer but an unbroken ring surrounding the harassed beast. For a few seconds longer the jackals stood watching and

waiting. Then one — the leader — moved forward, his body
crouched low.

The boar gave another grunt and tossed his head high
the vicious tusks gleaming in the moonlight.

That was the only challenge he offered. The next instant
those jackals at his rear were on him, leaping onto his back
and tearing at his flanks. He grunted once more and swayed
seeking to roll completely over to rid himself of the attackers

This proved to be the move that was to cost him his life
The leader of the pack had waited for just this one moment
Snaking in between the uplifted tusks, he managed to ge
the throat hold and closed his jaws.

The boar screamed with terror, then went down as the
remainder of the pack drove in on him. Thus did he die, a
sorely as had the shepherd bitch he had attacked on anothe
such night when the moon was high over the mountain.

When it was all over and the pack began to quarrel ove
the remains, the young dog withdrew from the scene, badly
frightened by their utter savagery. They still had paid no
attention to him, accepting him as one of themselves, and
because he wished not to attract attention, he continued to
move away from them.

The curiosity that had brought him away from the camp
fire of Saul, and had given him strength and fleetness of foo
to ascend once again the ramparts of the Hill of Hebron, no
longer sustained him. The singing in his blood had been
stilled, and in its place were the gentler influences of hi
mother.

Then suddenly eager to be off the mountain, while th

jackals still continued to worry their prey, he turned and fled, moving swiftly for fear of pursuit, knowing by instinct that the wild dogs of the hills, when gathered together in pack formation, were as deadly in their hunting as any boar.

Dawn found him crossing the ravine by way of the bridge of rubble, and the sun was well up before he came to the trail that struck down toward the distant fig tree and the far-off plain of the two rivers.

It was a much-chastened animal that came at last to the fig tree, and paused to stare up at it. For one brief second he thought it was another tree, and there seemed to be a figure hanging on it with arms outstretched.

Then the illusion vanished, and the dog knew it to be the same tree that had offered him shelter beneath its roots. The only thing different about it was the rude basket of sticks high up on its branches where the night bird had built its nest.

The dog remained close to the tree for the rest of the day, and by nightfall prepared to curl up amongst the roots as he had done in the days before he became the dog of the shepherd Saul.

He must have slept deeply, for he heard nothing, not even the sound of a stone falling down the slope, and he was very slow in waking when he became aware of hands touching him gently. Then opening his eyes, he looked up into the face of Saul, and in the moonlight it possessed all the kindness that had ever been expressed in the face of man throughout the ages.

The dog gave a broken whine, and the man gathered him

in his arms, and despite his size, carried him down the mountain as he would a lamb that had strayed, and laid him on a sheepskin rug before the campfire.

Happy and contented, the young dog slept unmoving, the turbulent singing in his blood stilled by the kindness of the man whom he knew to be his master and protector.

9: The Starlit Night

A FULL YEAR was spent by Saul, the shepherd, in the valley of the two rivers. In that time, the old dog, now heavy with the weight of the years, grew weary of the sheepherding, and one night his master found him dead, the younger animal watching over him. From that hour, the dog from the Hill of Hebron took over what had been the ancient one's rights, and the things he had learned from Saul he now tried to put to good purpose. There were times, however, when he would rebel and, obedient to the call of his blood, would wander off, being absent some two or three days. Always he came back, sometimes a sorry sight, happy to be just a dog again at the campfire of his master.

After seedtime in the second year of his sojourn in the valley of the two rivers, Saul became possessed with a yearning to go back to his own place, and by the seventh month, he was driving his flock along the ramparts of the mountains, making for Gath, in Judaea where, in his younger days, he had grazed his father's sheep.

By the ninth month, however, he had again taken to the hills, this time to the more austere heights above Bethlehem. It seemed that the solitude such as encountered on the hilltops, suited Saul's particular temperament admirably. As a result, he set out on his latest journey with a sense of extreme pleasure stirring in his heart and governing his every action.

While he was certainly regarded as a peculiar man amongst those who called themselves his neighbors, he was yet little different from the many others who herded sheep, and who had long since learned that solitude was good for the mind. It gave one the leisure to think and commune within oneself, learning afresh the things that, with the passing of youth, one had almost forgotten. More than that, being so much alone in the silent corridors of the hills, gave a shepherd confidence in himself, and a quiet assurance of how to conduct himself with others of his own kind who, through living so much alone, found speech difficult and therefore relied more upon a quick understanding than a ready tongue.

The dog, too, expressed great excitement at the new journey his master made up into the hills. Like the old dog, he had learned to interpret his master's wishes through a nod of the head rather than from word of mouth.

As both man and animal progressed farther up into the heights, he ran with waving tail and what, to Saul, were clearly laughing eyes.

To sights, sounds and smells, the animal responded effortlessly, enjoying to the utmost the feel of the wind on his back and the music it brought to his ears.

Saul and the dog had not been long on the heights above Bethlehem when the wind began to blow cold from the distant coast. With the welfare of his flock in mind, Saul brought both sheep and goats down to the scrub fields overlooking the Dead Sea where, with others of his mind, he prepared for the rainy season by building a hut in which to shelter.

As usual at that time of the year, the nights were bitterly cold. Thus Saul and his sheepherding companions found consolation by sitting huddled around their campfires for most of the hours of darkness.

One such night, a little colder than previously, found the shepherds even more closely huddled around their fires with the exception of Saul who, because of his contemplative nature, had drawn a little apart and was staring up at the stars. Never could he remember having seen them so bright. It seemed that the whole of the heavens was glowing with some hidden glory, one very large star standing out from the rest of the fiery host.

Even in his secret contemplation of the stars, and his partial withdrawal from the others, Saul yet heard them comment on the unusual brilliancy of the night.

He nodded quietly to himself, and fell to wondering.

Perhaps it was because their eyes were dazzled by the starlight, or maybe they were dreaming, but the shepherds and Saul thought that another had joined them — a stranger who stood outside the glow of the campfires. At the very instant they thought they saw him, they also thought they could hear the sound of distant singing — singing such as none of them could remember having heard before.

The moment was fraught with a strange fear that, gripping their hearts, held them speechless. The firelight flickered and cast sinuous fingers of flame in the direction of the shadow that stood without in the gloom. The voices, if voices there had been, had ceased to sing. It was exceedingly quiet. Nothing at all could be heard in the barren field, and only the sheep moved as they grazed, watched over by the patient, silent dogs.

Saul it was who roused himself first.

Moving in toward his companions, he said, 'Is it that we have been dreaming when we should have been awake, watching over our sheep?'

The note of inquiry in his voice failed to bring any response from the others. They were suddenly aware that with the movement of the old herdsman toward them, the shadow outside the glow of their campfires had vanished, and they were all wondering if it had ever been there at all, and whether Saul wasn't right when he asked if they had not all been dreaming instead of watching over their sheep.

Even so, in the pause that followed Saul's words, each man could still feel a little of the fear that had gripped his heart. More than that, some faint echo of the singing remained in their ears. Each man began to admit to himself that it was all very uncanny.

Then Saul, having no answer from his earlier inquiry, suggested that perhaps they should leave the sheep, and go down into the distant city to see if anything of importance was taking place.

'We can leave the dogs to guard the flocks,' he said.

'It is a good suggestion,' said one of the others, rising from his cramped position.

One by one, the shepherds left the campfires, and making a hasty patrol of the field were satisfied that the sheep were unlikely to wander far during their absence.

Even as they took their bearings, they could not fail to notice that the night was more brilliant than ever. Groups of stars, hitherto unknown to the shepherds, had become visible. The whole vault of the heavens was a palpitating blaze of light.

'It's a sign of great cold coming to us,' said one to Saul.

The old man nodded, suddenly shivering.

He then called his dog over to him and, indicating his own sheep, bade him remain on guard.

A few minutes later, Saul and his companions departed, walking slowly across the field. Reaching the barren hillside, they set off on the long journey to the distant city.

For a long while after Saul's departure, the young dog lay watching the slow movement of the sheep as they cropped the coarse grass. The patient creatures trod pace after pace from one spot to another, all keeping together, the lambs with the ewes as if bound by an inseparable bond.

The night still continued exceedingly bright. The dog could distinguish clearly the rough walls of stone that marked the limits of the grazing, and away off by the eastern gate, the uprising rock finger that was often used as a rubbing post by sheep and goats alike.

Suddenly the dog felt restless. Welling up in him was a desire to follow his master despite the order to remain with the flock. It was no insistent urge to wander off into the high hills as on those other occasions when he had forsaken the sheep. This time, it was a quieter, more subtle desire to follow his master.

He whined nervously. Although the memory remained

of those other occasions when he had disobeyed Saul, he had never done so when the sheep had been left in his charge. Now, just when he should be unswervingly obedient to his master's wishes, since Saul himself had gone off, there was this urge to go out of the field and across the hill slope, and it was an urge that had its being in a new and joyous singing of the blood in his veins.

Twice the young dog patrolled the field to satisfy himself that the sheep were perfectly safe and disinclined to stray. On each occasion he noticed the other dogs — also put on guard by their masters — lying contentedly within marshaling distance of their flocks. It was obvious to the younger animal that they, at least, were not disturbed by some unfulfilled desire. They appeared as calm as the sheep they watched over.

At last the young dog could no longer resist. He suddenly went like a shadow across the barren field and on to the greater barrenness of the hillside.

Once outside the rudely constructed walls, he stood on the ill-defined sheep track, his tail feathered, his ears sharply erect.

The brightness that had been characteristic of the field was not quite so obvious on the hill. The stars above continued to shine extraordinarily bright, but actual visibility on the hill was little more than a few yards. Beyond that, due to the many depressions that went from north to south of the escarpment, it was quite gloomy.

The dog, however, was in no way disconcerted. Since he traveled more by scent than by sight, the darkness did not deter him. Putting his nose to the ground, he rapidly picked up his master's scent, and set off at an easy loping pace. There were moments when he paused, testing the atmosphere. Otherwise he kept on the move.

A star that had been the evening star, was going slowly down the sky when the dog finally approached the city. Even as he set foot within the city walls, the star waned and was no more. Only a lone bird, flying as a falcon flies, saw it flicker and burn out as does a fire whose little hour is spent and done.

10: Let His Name Be Petrus

THE DOG had a little difficulty in following his master's scent through the mean city streets, and although the night was now far spent, there were still a few belated travelers abroad to confuse him. Nevertheless, he managed to keep hard on the trail of Saul, and came at last to an inn where a small party of late arrivals had started to argue with the innkeeper who had no shelter to offer.

By the constant use of his nose, the dog knew that his master was not at the inn, and moving forward slowly with his muzzle to the ground, he came at last to a stable.

The door stood open, and the yellow glow of lamplight spilled out into the meager courtyard and the night. In the gloom, the eaves of the building slanted upward and away from sight.

Voices, quiet and subdued, filtered out into the courtyard and at the sound of them, the dog, who stood watching and listening, pricked his ears. He recognized the tones of his master.

It was a moment such as had never before come to an animal of his kind — a moment almost as great as that which had come a little earlier to the cattle and an ass that were housed in the stable.

Then, like the sheep, which but a short while before the dog had watched, moving pace by pace as they grazed, so did the animal without a name move, stiff-legged and hesitant, step by step toward the open door and the warm glow of lamplight within. Only when he stood at the very threshold did he stop, gazing in with wondering eyes at the scene.

An ass stood in a stall munching hay. In stalls on either side were patient-eyed cattle, chewing contentedly and quietly swishing their tails from side to side. A wavering light from a lantern swinging from a beam cast heavy shadows that moved as did the lantern itself, revealing for one short second an hitherto hidden corner, then a stack of hay and some leather water bags.

No shadow, however, fell where the Babe lay happily in a manger, no shadow either where Mary, His mother, and Joseph, her spouse, acknowledged the shepherds' gently uttered words of greeting.

The dog on the threshold made no attempt to enter; he just gazed with eyes bright with wonder, like one seeing far into the future that was beyond the reach of the strongest wind and the farthest sea and all that moved on the waves thereof. His vision took in at a single glance the violence of a multitude gathered to do injury to One who had come amongst them; his nostrils even held for an instant the acrid scent of dust and blood, and then the scent of dew in the early morning, with voices singing.

These things, and more, the dog saw in that inward searching glance into events that were yet unborn . . . the old fig tree was in the vision too . . . the tree no longer withered and old, but young, with a wondrous flowering amongst its branches and the birds of the air dwelling at peace in the shade.

He suddenly whined.

Saul turned sharply at the sound, his face expressing anger at sight of the dog he had bidden to remain in the field and keep watch over the sheep.

Like one of the great multitude in the vision he had just glimpsed, the animal saw his master raise high his herding crook to bring it down on his back.

He crouched low to the ground, his eyes appealing in their acute distress, his ears pressed flat against his skull and his back already quivering at the sharpness of the blow he could all but feel.

The crook remained poised over him, casting a broken shadow over his head and flanks. Saul's hand was arrested by the voice of Mary speaking softly, saying, 'Be not angry with him. Do him no injury, for he, too, would look upon my Babe!'

With unutterable tenderness she surveyed the cringing animal. She thrust forth one hand from beneath her robe.

'Come!' she said.

Very gently the dog obeyed her command, crossing the threshold and moving past Saul, his master, until he lay at Mary's feet, looking up at her with eyes soft with humility.

The ass and the cattle regarded him with a sense of kinship.

Mary asked Saul how the dog was called.

The shepherd shook his head ruefully.

'He has no name,' he answered.

Mary lowered her hand to caress the animal's head, Joseph

smiling tenderly as her fingers encountered the dog's nose
which was moist and cold.

Smiling back at Joseph, and then at Saul, she remarked,
'He should be called "Petrus," for his nose is cold like a
stone that has lain long in the river.'

Mary then turned to the manger.

Joseph, interpreting her wishes, placed the Holy Babe in
her arms.

With the surpassing tenderness of all women in her
glance, she raised the Holy Child, holding Him firm against
her shoulder. In that instant, before the shepherds and the
cattle, and the ass that had so patiently carried her from
Galilee to this town of Bethlehem, and the dog who lay
watchful at her feet, she became the Mother of All Living,
and her Child, the symbol of what all children should be to
mothers whose arms must always hold them and keep them
safe.

Perhaps he slept — that Holy Child! But no! His eyes
opened, and He looked down upon the dog who had come
with the shepherds to do Him homage — this dog who,
from henceforth was to be known as 'Petrus — the dog whose
nose was cold like a stone.'

There was a deep silence in the stable. The ass and the
cattle had ceased their chewing, and it seemed that the night
sounds outside had also been suddenly stilled. Only the
lantern, caught by a frail trickle of wind, swung more inces-
santly to and fro, causing the shadows to pass and repass
with greater insistence over the soiled floor of the stable and
over the prone shape of the dog who looked with peace upon
the Infant Christ.

Almost like a promise for that future he had glimpsed but a few minutes before, there was born in the dog an orientation, the fulfilment of which was to be a happy augury for all animals. In it lay the destiny that, in the years ahead, would uplift all animals and bring them closer to man; for Petrus was, in due time, to become the one creature who, despite affliction, was to remain constant to one master unto the end.

Soon the shepherds took their leave of the Holy Family, and departed into the night to rejoin their flocks, traveling now joyful at heart and remembering all that they had seen that night. At their heels trotted the dog Petrus, his head held high, his tail plumed, and his eyes soft with the light of understanding. It was plain to the shepherds, and to Saul, that the dog would give willing service to man. How could they know that as they saw him now — young and virile — so would he be in the years ahead, with no sign of age upon him?

Thus, still marveling at all they had seen, the shepherds came at last to the barren field where their sheep were still peaceably grazing.

They stared in wonder.

Behold, in the field they thought barren, how great a glory the late-rising moon revealed! As Petrus passed amongst the stones, starry blossoms sprang where the press of his feet had been.

Indeed, behold the field — the once barren field! No greater glory could any field possess than that which the moon revealed on this night when the shepherds returned to their flocks after visiting the lowly stable in Bethlehem, and the dog Petrus whom the Holy Child had looked upon passed like a shadow before them!

The shepherds and Saul knew then that Petrus was the most favored of animals; and with him, they remained in the field many days, and did eat only of the flowers and herbs of the field.

PART TWO

Within the Shadow
of the Robe

11: The Dog of the Shepherd Saul

FROM THE Plain of Sharon and across the Valley of Jezreel, even far into Galilee, dogs had never been held in high esteem. They were considered bad and unreliable, and while some were kept for protection against thieves and the like, they were seldom, if ever, permitted within the household, but stayed in the courtyards, and slept for the most part without a roof over their heads.

Saul, the shepherd, who had always kept and cared for dogs, was considered eccentric by his neighbors. The very fact that he had for years succeeded in training dogs to assist with his sheep only added to this opinion of him.

True there were other shepherds who took dogs with them to protect the flocks from marauding jackals and wild boars, but it was seldom indeed they were used in the way adopted by Saul.

Thus, in a community where the very name 'dog' was used as a word of scorn or insult, Saul's acceptance of Petrus as a constant companion was regarded as further evidence of eccentric behavior. It had been bad enough when he had merely kept a dog to care for and protect the sheep, but to have one forever at his heels was something his companions could not understand.

It was, they all were apt to declare with a shake of their

heads, a sure sign that Saul was becoming old indeed. Some conjectured as to how much longer the herdsman would be able to go into the lonely places of the hills with his sheep, for he always traveled farther than any of the other shepherds to find the choicest grazing for his flocks.

Saul, knowing much that was being said about him, held his peace, and merely looked upon Petrus with something now closely akin to affection.

It was perhaps a pity those herdsmen who had been his companions on that memorable night had long since returned to their own place. They, of all men, had surely understood the strange happenings of that night, and of the new place the dog Petrus had in Saul's heart.

Because of this, and maybe the knowledge that from the very hour the Infant Jesus looked upon him, the dog had changed in both manner and bearing, and seemed possessed of much wisdom and understanding, Saul cared not what his neighbors said or thought of him.

Amongst other things, which for most men would have been of the first importance, the dog had become a most expert herder of sheep. As a result Saul could now sleep quietly at night, sure in the knowledge that his flock was closely guarded.

Toward the approach of the rainless season, Saul made one of those decisions for which he had become the despair of many another shepherd. He decided to drive his sheep across the Valley of Jezreel and up into the rich green plain of Sharon. It was his desire to make for the small river that rose up on the heights of Mount Gerizim. The grazing, under the very shadow of the mountain, was said to be ex-

ceptionally good for most of the dry season. Confident that
the journey could be safely undertaken with so excellent a
dog as Petrus to keep the flock on the move, Saul set off, after
making preparations for a trek likely to last for many days.

The journey through the Valley of Jezreel and up toward
the hill country situated at the head of two rivers, was certainly accomplished in good time and without a single sheep
being lost. Once around the northwestern foothills, and
within a few miles of Samaria, trouble overtook Saul. Both
he and his flock were threatened by thieves come down from
Gilead way across the Jordan Valley.

As was so often the pattern, the attack was made without
warning, the night having come, and there being no moon
to reveal the presence of the thieves.

Saul had driven his sheep into a grassy acclivity bordered
on the south by a rocky escarpment. His camp was set up
within the confines of an overspill of boulder and scree,
where a patch of moss made for comfort such as the herdsman felt he needed after being so long on the journey.

The day was long a-dying in the west. Indeed, the afterglow still lingered over the hill country south of Phoenicia.
The great mountain plain thrusting up beyond Capernaum
in Galilee, was like an enormous shadow. Over its more
western ramparts, the sunset trembled and blazed with
color. Tenuous fingers of light reached out, broke where
some small hill impeded it, and only again found reflection
where a fissure allowed the almost liquid color to filter
through.

Petrus was very much on the alert. Not a single ewe
moved but that he knew of it, nor did a lamb run bleating

through the scrub, without he marked its progress and stood
poised to see that it came to no harm.

Saul, watching him through half-closed eyes, marveled
at the handsome animal he had become. Once when Petrus
stood on an outcrop of rock, silhouetted against the fast-
dying light of day, the shepherd studied him most closely.

Nodding his head slowly, Saul gave a sigh of great pleasure. The dog had certainly grown into something quite
unlike the usual pariah dog so often seen carrying out the
duties of herding.

There was now, at first sight, little about him of the shepherd bitch who had been his mother. He was, when alert,
more like the wild dog, his sire, but possessed none of that
animal's vicious attributes.

His back was straight and lacked the cringing slope that
characterized the outcasts of the canine race. Moreover, he
was high in the leg, with a sturdy neck that matched the
firmly set body. His head was broad, the muzzle tapering
to clean-cut jaws. His ears, like those of a wolf, or wild dog,
were erect, and gave a definite nobility of bearing that would
have been hard to find in any other dog either in Judaea or
Galilee. His fine bushy tail, now raised to the level of his
back, gave the final distinction to what was clearly an animal
such as Saul had never known before.

The afterglow was now little more than a wavering pattern of color over the mountain plain of the west; the first
stars were rising and the dusk coming up over the flanks of
the hills.

Shivering, because the air was growing cold, the old herdsman drew his robe tightly about him. Throwing more scrub

onto the fire, he settled himself as comfortably as he could into the mossy hollow he had chosen for his bed.

Abruptly Petrus swung about, facing the cliffs rising above him. He remained very still, listening.

All the primitive instincts of the wild dog who had been his sire were alive in him then. There was a trickle of wind coming down from off the hills, and the man scent was strong in it.

As his nostrils widened to take in the scent, so did the hair on his neck and back stiffen. In another moment, he was crouching low to the ground and, sliding off the outcrop, made for a gully along which he began to crawl.

Meanwhile, Saul had dozed off and was unaware that anything was amiss. The fire flickered and burned low; the darkness deepened. Only the scent of wood smoke hovered in the night air.

Suddenly there was a shout far up the hill, and a man who had been lying stretched out on the ground, the better to observe the dark movement of Saul's sheep, found himself menaced by some creature he could not readily identify. There had been no sign, no sound. He had half raised himself when the creature came at him, and in his fear he cried out, rousing his three companions who were scattered up the hillside.

Mistaking this for a sign to go in, attack Saul and steal his sheep, they jumped out of their hiding places and ran shouting down the slope. Like his companion before him, the first of the three men, who was well in the lead, had no idea what struck him. All he beheld was a dark shape rising up at his very feet. The shadow took on a substance that, on

impact, sent him hurtling backward. It was at this same
moment that the thief already menaced by Petrus went running off along a ridge, shouting in a loud voice that a wild
beast was at large on the mountain.

Meanwhile, Saul, roused by the shouting and screaming,
rose hastily and ran out to ensure that none of his sheep took
fright and made off.

By now, the remaining thieves were losing confidence in
the venture. The men already harassed by the dog were running back along the main ridge to the track that led across
the mountain massif to the distant Jordan Valley.

Their constant shouting caused the others to pause uncertainly. As the foremost man turned to glance up at the
skyline against which the ridge was sharply defined, he
glimpsed two figures moving rapidly in the direction of the
trail. He, too, turned about to clamber back along the route
he had followed. Like the others, he was thrown off balance
by the violent impact of something attacking him from the
rear.

He put out his hands to save himself. As he fell, striking
his head, he was aware of a shape hastening off after the remaining thief, who had paused in panic.

It was this fellow who afterward made an attempt to
describe the animal to his companions. It was a wild dog,
he said, coming up at him with a strange light in its eyes,
and with white fangs gleaming against a red tongue.

Nobody thought of questioning how he could have seen
the animal of which he told, though by that time it had
become quite dark on the hill. All they did know was that

the picture they themselves had allowed to grow up in their minds was somehow the same.

They hesitated no longer on the escarpment, but made off as quickly as they could, swearing that the mountain was the abode of devils that hunted at nightfall accompanied by a beast as large as any boar, and twice as deadly.

Not one of them marveled that they had escaped without injury. They had only been overthrown and badly shaken, the very swiftness of the encounter being sufficient to rouse them to terror, and afterward to conjecture as to what nature of creature it was that inhabited the mountain.

The fame of his exploit that night on the heights of Samaria was noised abroad amongst the herdsmen and their families. Since Saul had not lost any of his ewes or lambs, and no man had come into one of the villages to have his wounds dressed, there were many who doubted that the attack had ever taken place.

It was, many were wont to declare, but another instance of the old shepherd's crazy notions about the activities of the dog he had trained to protect his sheep. Others merely shook their heads, and wondered. Many strange things were happening throughout the land. The exploits of the dog, Petrus, were the least important of them.

By seedtime, Saul was far away, having returned to the area of the two rivers that rose on the heights of the southern hills about Beersheba.

The very ancient fig tree that had been nigh to dying and beneath which Petrus had once rested, was now full of sap, and exceedingly green. The birds of the air nested in its

branches, and the place about it was fragrant like a paradise
for all wild things that sought refuge from those that hunted
their kind on the hills above.

Petrus came to it but once that season, and then only to
gaze upon the spot where he had rested, and slept.

12: Petrus and the Child Martha

PETRUS, IN his third year, seemed to have changed very little. He had achieved early maturity, and with it strength and courage seldom seen in animals that lacked confidence because they were still the scorn of all small communities. By now, he had become so familiar a sight with Saul that folk ceased to sneer. Certainly none of Saul's acquaintances but regarded the dog as something the shepherd could well be proud of. There were even some among them who harbored thoughts of stealing the dog. What deterred them was that they all remembered the many tales told of the animal's exploits on the hills. Maybe he would give too good an account of himself if suddenly seized.

Also Petrus had, in the past year, become well known. His fame had traveled far beyond Galilee and Phoenicia, even to the wild country of Philippi.

To be branded as a thief in the eyes of all rendered one unworthy of succor and shelter in time of need. Since these were years of trouble and tribulation for all in Cana of Galilee, when no man could be sure of what the future might bring, it did not behoove any to bring the contempt of his neighbors upon himself.

Meanwhile, the days of fulfilment had come to the land, and after many anxieties it was found that the harvest was good. Sharing his joys with the husbandmen was Saul, for from his long sojourn in the valley of the two rivers he returned to his own place with a fine flock of young lambs. These he had sold for more pieces of silver than he could ever before remember possessing.

This was the time when the shepherd usually took his ease in his brother-in-law's house a few miles from Nain in the Valley of Jezreel. The brother-in-law, Jacob, was one of those who would have liked Petrus as his own animal. Naomi, his wife and the sister of Saul, knew this and distrusted her husband's thoughts and sudden solicitude for the shepherd.

She liked to have her brother with her after his long periods away, but on this occasion she began to have fears for him. Jacob, often home early from the vineyards, sat at the door of their humble dwelling watching the antics of Petrus with the children in the village.

It was odd, Jacob thought moodily, how so huge an animal could yet be so tender and gentle with children. Petrus, unlike others of his kind, simply loved to lie in the dust of the street while the children romped over him, pulling at his fur and ofttimes tweaking his ears.

One child, more venturesome than the rest, was a special favorite with him. She was Martha, the daughter of one Deborah, who had come from Egypt. Martha was dark like her mother, and as vivacious. Her years were but seven. Each morning, soon after sunup, she would come to the house of Naomi and Jacob, demanding to see Petrus.

Since the animal was not permitted in the house but was presumed to sleep in the stable at the rear, Jacob complained

The children romped over him

to his wife that the child need not come to the house for Petrus. It was then, after Martha continued to make her morning calls, that Jacob discovered occasions when Saul smuggled the animal into his small sleeping apartment.

This Jacob regarded as an affront to his hospitality, and, moreover, since he and Naomi were childless, and the child's repeated presence reminded him of the fact, he was moved to anger against his brother-in-law.

The hour was fast approaching, however, when Saul would be getting together another flock of ewes and rams and setting off into the hills.

On the last night of Saul's stay, the child Martha and Petrus went out in the cool of the evening, wandering far from the village and down into the plain toward the valley of the river. It was a rich green place in which they tarried while the sunset flamed and died in the west. There was the sound of bird song, and some ravens, returning late to their nests on the crags of Mount Gilboa, called hoarsely as they flew high overhead.

Petrus was becoming anxious. He sensed that Martha should not be so far from her home, with night gathering over the plain. He constantly encircled the child, nuzzling her and endeavoring to get her to retrace her steps in the direction of the village. She had, however, discovered a place where small white flowers grew in abundance, and she was too engrossed in gathering them to notice that the light was fast draining from the sky. It was not until the moon began to rise and a wild dog barked afar off that she became frightened and looked to Petrus for protection.

The animal nuzzled her once again, and this time, be-

:ause of her fear, Martha caught hold of the hide collar Saul
1ad placed about the dog's neck. Petrus then turned toward
1ome, leading Martha gently so they could both travel easily
he narrow path that wandered across the valley. More than
)nce the child stumbled, her sandaled feet being unfamiliar
with the way she trod. When at last she began to cry, Petrus
ried as best he could to comfort her.

By now it was quite dark, with only the moon for light.
The far-off baying of the wild dogs possessed a deeper and
more sinister significance.

Petrus essayed to quicken his pace a little, but Martha
was tired and very much frightened.

The dog was in no doubt as to the way he should travel
o reach the village. Even so, there was a growing apprehen-
ion in him for the safety of the child. The baying of the
)ariah dogs was coming closer. Knowing them for what they
were, Petrus knew that he could not fight and subdue them
ill if by chance they were in a pack and led by an experi-
:nced leader.

Notwithstanding his anxiety, Petrus kept up a steady
)ace, treading carefully so that Martha could keep up with
1im, her fingers still clutching hold of the hide collar about
1is neck. Once he half turned his head in an effort to lick
1er fingers and reassure her; often he paused so she could
egain her breath and lean against him. It seemed that in
:his hour of a child's great need, all knowledge was his, and
ill love.

It had grown quite cold, the heat of the day suddenly
leparting when night had finally come. The stars were hard
ind exceedingly bright, and there was a nimbus around the

moon denoting the possibility of a ground frost before another hour was past.

Martha, clad only in light clothes, began to feel the cold to such an extent that this, too, added to her dejection and fear. All the stories she had heard of the strange beasts that inhabited the lonely places of the earth, kept recurring. She thought she could see many of them, standing out in the darkness waiting to destroy her and Petrus.

At last she could not keep back the sudden wave of terror that assailed her. She began to cry loudly, calling upon one name to help her, 'Petrus — Petrus!'

The dog stood close beside her, looking up into her face, and trying to guide her onward to home and safety. She was so utterly weary that her legs could scarcely support her. Then when she unexpectedly fell, striking herself against a large stone, her crying took on a more terrified note.

Her fingers had lost their hold on the dog's collar, and for one short second she felt herself to be completely alone. Another second, short in the eternity of time the plain had known, but very long in the life of the child Martha, and Petrus had swung about, sniffing her anxiously, a broken whine in his throat.

The child ceased her crying, staring upward at the dog. Her eyes were stark with the fear she felt, her hands reaching up to touch him, sensing that only with him did her safety lie.

Petrus was bristling. Less than a score of yards away, an animal bayed out loud and clear. He was answered by others from a little way out in the plain.

It seemed then that where the wild dogs crouched, wait

ng, the night was darkest. Not one of them was revealed to Petrus, who stood alert, trying to locate them.

Although he could not see them, Petrus knew full well that the wild brothers, with whom he no longer possessed any sense of kinship, were gathering for the final hunting down of himself and Martha.

He took up a stance over the prostrate child. He then added his own voice to the chorus of sounds that were rising from out of the darkness. In his bark, however, was a challenge, a challenge to those who threatened the child he was determined to protect. As he continued to bark, he sought also to attract help from the village which he knew instinctively was now not too far off.

The small party of men, who were already out searching for the missing child, heard, echoing above the now increased baying of the wild dogs, the deep-throated bark of the animal they knew to be Petrus.

They took bearings from the sound, and with anxiety in their hearts, hastened in its direction.

When it first was known that Martha was not in the village, and that Petrus, too, was missing, Jacob complained to Naomi and Deborah, saying that the dog lacked proper supervision, and should be subject to a master other than Saul, who permitted him to do just as he liked.

Naomi, discerning the meaning of her husband's remarks, remonstrated with him, saying that Petrus was an excellent dog and that Martha would come to no harm while in his company.

Deborah was inclined to agree with her, but when night

had come and the child and the dog had not returned, she became very frightened. Search parties were formed to scour the plain.

Jacob continued more strongly than ever to voice his opinions. He kept saying that this would never have happened if Petrus had been kept under better control by his master. Were he the owner, the dog would be kept on a chain in the yard and not permitted to roam the village to the annoyance of his neighbors.

Moreover, he said, his brother-in-law was much too old to continue with the herding of sheep. Now that the herdsman had a reasonable sum of money, he should give up the herding, live quietly with himself and Naomi, and hand over the dog, who could be put to another use.

It was a pity that Saul was not with his brother-in-law's party to hear what was being proposed for his future. As it was, he and a half dozen others were in another part of the plain. Saul recognized the bark of Petrus the instant the animal gave tongue.

The herdsman turned to his companions, saying that Petrus could not be more than half a mile away to the south.

The men agreed with him and immediately set off to cover the distance to where Petrus stood over the child, defying the wild dogs. Saul it was who reached the scene first and not a moment too soon!

Moving quietly, and crouching low to the ground, the pack had closed in, and had all but encircled the helpless child and the dog.

Petrus could now see the animals' eyes gleaming and

discern their crouching shapes less than a dozen yards away.

He was fully prepared to fight them all, and indeed his lips were drawn back in a snarl of defiance that showed only too clearly that he was willing to surrender his life in an effort to save Martha from their fangs. Just when it seemed that the pack was assembled to attack in a mass and Petrus must be overthrown, there was a shout.

Saul and his friends came running up out of the night. The wild dogs hesitated, bristling with mingled fear and anger before making off across the plain, their fear of man being greater than their desire to kill.

When Jacob and his party arrived on the scene, Martha was safe in the arms of Saul, while Petrus was sitting on his haunches, looking up into his master's face. Before Jacob could make any appropriate comment, he heard Martha say that Petrus was a very good dog. He had stood guard over her, keeping her safe from the animals who had wanted to kill her.

Jacob looked first at Petrus, then at the child herself, who still clutched the white flowers she had gathered. He looked, too, upon the bowed head of his brother-in-law, and for some quite unknown reason, was aware of a deep regret for what he had said earlier to those who had come with him.

As this wave of regret continued to well up in him, he realized, with surprise, that he no longer resented his brother-in-law having Petrus as a constant companion. He sensed, vaguely, that it was possibly compensation for so many other things the old man did not possess. In that moment of revelation he glimpsed much he had not known.

He came to understand that he had far less cause to be dissatisfied than he had hitherto imagined, even though he and Naomi were childless.

He was, after all, well set up in his trade as chandler, and held in respect by many because he was a master man. His vineyards were prosperous. As for the fact that he possessed no child of his own, maybe the time would yet come when Naomi would present him with a son or daughter. If not, there were still orphans abroad, one of whom might well assuage the ache in his heart, even if not of his own flesh and blood.

When a little later the whole party was set on the path leading straight to the village, Saul strode on ahead of the others with Martha asleep in his arms and Petrus walking quietly at his heels.

Behind them, way out across the Valley of Jezreel, the gloom was little more than a curious half-light, for the moon was riding in a cloudless sky. In the small drinking pools much sought after by cattle, a few stars winked, while the moon itself found reflection where the water lay very quiet and unruffled.

No wild dog bayed now; no night bird passed in questing flight over the river. A little wind that had come in from the sea had gone like the breath of a sigh, scarcely disturbing the salt crystals that gleamed on the reeds that rose like lances, white-tipped, toward the sky.

A very peaceful night, the events of the early evening being little more than a memory, to be completely lost when a new day dawned.

13: No Larger Than a Man's Hand

SAUL'S JOURNEY to the proposed new grazing in the Jordan River Valley was well underway a week later. He had acquired from a trader in Nain a new flock of some twenty ewes, together with a few rams and one goat. With Petrus keeping the flock under constant surveillance, Saul entered the valley with a measure of satisfaction in his heart. Things had gone so well with him so far that he considered himself a most favored man indeed.

The grazing at the approaches to the valley was rough in the extreme, being sparse and interspersed with scrub. However, a little before sundown, the river was within sight, and Saul decided not to pitch his camp until he was out of the area of scrub.

He therefore indicated to Petrus that he desired to press on, and the dog, understanding his gestures, ran in widening circles around the sheep, keeping them on the move.

At last, when night had come, the flock was scattered over a strip of pasture enclosed in the north by the main part of the river that flowed down the Valley of Jezreel to the sea, and in the west by the fork that flowed through Descapolis to the Sea of Galilee.

Saul set up his small tent happy in the knowledge that he reached thus far without mishap. He then kindled his

campfire. After a supper of goat's milk and bread, he prepared himself for sleep, aware that Petrus, who slept just
outside the tent, would keep guard.

The old shepherd had noticed that a little wind had risen
with the going down of the sun, but he did not pay much
attention to it. Only an hour or so after midnight, when it
was blowing stronger and Saul awakened for a brief span,
did he consider that it was a wind that smelled strongly of
the sea.

Even so, he was exceedingly weary, and before he could
determine whether or not the wind might foretell a spell of
very bad weather, he was asleep once more, not waking again
before the sun was well up above the heights of Judaea.

Petrus, meanwhile, had got the sheep grazing in a sheltered spot where Mount Gilboa broke the strong flow of the
wind. The dog himself lay on a small hillock, watching the
flock with a keenness that gave Saul the utmost satisfaction.

Suddenly the herdsman shivered. He realized that it was
very cold. Acting on an impulse, he shaded his eyes and
gazed over the foothills to the summit of Mount Gilboa. He
was surprised to see a drift of cloud breaking over the mountain like smoke. After it had streamed away and the sky
beyond was visible, he saw, almost stationary, a cloud no
larger than the palm of a man's hand.

What Saul could not understand was that, while the mist
had gone flying away on what was clearly a strong current
of air, the cloud remained absolutely motionless, as if held in
a vacuum.

Since the mist had gone and there was no other cloud in
the sky, he regarded the phenomenon without any sense

of apprehension. Moreover, because he had kept the sheep constantly on the move since leaving Nain, he decided to remain a few days on the western side of the river, crossing by the only fording point the day following the Sabbath.

The next two days found the shepherd taking his ease. He contented himself with making a new pair of sandals from some dried goatskin he had brought with him for the purpose. All this time, the wind continued to come in strongly from the sea, and the cloud that had been no larger than the palm of a man's hand still remained motionless over Mount Gilboa. The only ominous thing about it was that it appeared to have become a little larger. On the afternoon before the Sabbath, Saul, glancing up at it, experienced a stab of alarm.

It seemed to be not quite so high in the sky, and was burning dun-colored in the light of the sunset.

Saul slept fitfully that night, and next day he was compelled to keep within his tent, for the wind was sharp like a knife. The sheep were huddled together for protection, while the goat had come in close to the tent, seeking more congenial companionship in the shape of Petrus, who lay close to the fire.

The shepherd was awake early next day, determined to get the sheep over to the opposite bank of the river. He felt that before long that ominous cloud would break in torrential rain, and he was anxious to reach higher ground. Adjacent to the northern mountain range there would be deeply recessed valleys to offer greater protection should the weather continue uncertain.

He breakfasted and stamped out the campfire while

Petrus ate his full morning meal of goat's milk and dried crusts. Just before he took down the tent, Saul gave the dog a goodly supply of meat, for he felt that before the day was out the animal's strength would be sorely tried. Petrus, surprised at this additional supply of rations, ate it with relish before awaiting his master's commands for work.

Everything was in readiness. The tent and the small domestic utensils had been packed neatly so as to present no difficulty when the old man himself followed the sheep across the river.

In no time, Saul and the dog were marshaling the sheep, driving them toward the loop in the river where a sizable sand bar made a crossing reasonably safe. At one or two places there was scarcely any water at all, and provided the leading rams kept a straight course, the entire flock could be got across within an hour at most.

The movement was well under way when Saul heard coming in from the north the deep roll of thunder. He glanced up at the cloud that for many days had been held motionless over Mount Gilboa. He was startled that it had increased ominously, and was now on the very summit of the mountain.

Suddenly flashes of lightning pierced it from end to end, and the voice of the thunder traveled steadily nearer.

As a general rule, Saul was a most cautious man, and at another time might well have taken heed of the warnings that were being so strikingly conveyed to him. On this particular day, however, he was a deal less prudent than the occasion demanded. He was driven with the desire to press on at all costs and get his sheep onto the eastern bank of the river.

Petrus worked with a will. Saul, directing operations, gave but one or two significant whistles which the dog understood, and for the rest Petrus worked instinctively. The rams began to go into the lead and, with Petrus running alongside them, arrived without hesitation at the fording point.

The flow of water was quite steady as the sheep gathered to make the crossing. Saul, glancing up once again at the cloud, was still undismayed and persisted in his endeavor to drive the flock across the sand bar without delay.

No sooner had the first of the sheep stepped onto the sand bar than a terrific crash of thunder reverberated up the whole of the Jordan Valley, and came resounding back as the deep report met the opposing barrier of the mountains of Gilead. At the same instant, the cloud over Mount Gilboa broke up in torrential rain. Water rolled down the foothills, filling every gully and ravine. In a matter of seconds, the river itself began to rise, and way up the Jordan Valley, a white line of foam coursed down in the direction of the sand bar.

Saul realized too late that he should have waited until the threatened storm had broken and thrashed itself out. He could then have remained safe on the western bank, exposed no doubt to the brunt of the rain, but without having to face the hazards that must now accompany a crossing of the river.

It was, of course, much too late to draw back now. The crossing just had to be made.

The sheep were becoming frightened. Fortunately, the rams, already well out on the sand bar, were hastening their steps as if fully aware that only on the opposite bank could they expect to be safe from the approaching wall of water.

Saul was running to the rear of the flock, and Petrus, acting now without any instructions stood out in the river with the rising water washing over his flanks and back. He was trying to keep the sheep from breaking formation, indicating the direction they should take by edging himself slowly forward along the crumbling edges of the sand bar.

Bleating with terror, the now thoroughly terrified creatures hastened after the rams. Indeed, half the flock was across before the agitated currents began to wash over the lower portions of the causeway.

Petrus was now forced to tread water, managing to keep his head well up and watching closely those ewes that disclosed greater signs of terror than the others. In this moment of great need the dog had no thought of himself and the danger he was in. His only consideration was for the sheep his master expected him to safeguard.

Thus, when one of the ewes found herself caught by an unexpected wave and swept off her feet, Petrus was near at hand to help her. Quick though the dog was, the wave was stronger than he had anticipated and the ewe was rapidly tossed into a downward surge of water that carried her into the main flow of the river currents.

Petrus swung away from the sand bar and struck out after her. By now the causeway was breaking up. The dog struggled valiantly against the tawny torrent, finally reaching the struggling ewe.

With a swift plunge forward, Petrus managed to grip her by the loose wool about the neck. The ewe, by now much too terrified to struggle further, felt herself being propelled toward the bank by Petrus, who was swimming powerfully against the breaking torrent of sand and water.

Saul, meanwhile, was hustling the last of the flock across what remained of the sand bar. With his staff much in evidence, he finally succeeded in getting the last ewe off the causeway, and turned his attention to Petrus.

The rain was falling like a gray wall of water. The shepherd could scarcely see through it. Then he heard a bark and saw Petrus standing less than a dozen yards away, shaking himself. At his feet lay the ewe, panting heavily, but nonetheless alive!

With a prayer in his heart because the dog had survived the terrible ordeal, Saul ran to give succor to the distressed ewe. She was not long in recovering and hastened off, bleating. Not long afterward the whole flock, including the goat that had reached safety in advance of the rams, roamed about in search of pasture. The danger they had all so recently experienced was forgotten in the immediate need for food.

Saul, regardless of the torrential rain, then knelt before Petrus, running his fingers through the animal's wet fur. 'Ye've been a courageous dog,' he said quietly, and was rewarded by the animal licking his hand. He looked long and searchingly into the dog's eyes, and in their depths discerned the great affection Petrus had for him.

He was still savoring his pleasure at the thought when the white ridge of foam from far up the river came thrusting at the remains of the sand bar. In less than a minute the fording place was gone. It had completely broken up and vanished in a muddy surge toward the main flow of the river going down to the sea.

Saul shook his head, again thankful at their escape. He then proceeded, with the continued aid of Petrus, to drive the sheep to the high ground where, in a ravine surrounded with lofty cliffs, they found shelter from the fierce drive of both wind and rain. There he attempted to dry off the dog's coat.

This was the havoc wrought by the cloud no larger at first than the palm of a man's hand.

That night, far over in the Jordan River basin, the wild dogs and boars hunted. Oxen overtaken by the flood water had died, and their carcasses afforded much feasting for those who inhabited the wild. Famine that had existed for many days was, on this night following the cloudburst over Mount Gilboa, at an end.

As for Saul, he was so utterly weary that despite the oft-repeated calls up the entire length of the valley, he slept the heavy sleep of a man exhausted by the efforts he has made to save those under his care. Petrus, however, who had so nobly aided him in his endeavors, did not sleep. For him, those distant calls of the hunters spoke of possible danger to the sheep.

He remained alert throughout the night, sheltering against the onslaught of the rain where a rocky overhang gave him a little protection.

By daybreak, the rain was drifting away to the mountains of Gilead, and with it went the night hunters, to sleep in their caves where man did not come and deep darkness hid them from the eyes of those who might destroy them.

14: The Lamb That Was Lost

PETRUS WAS a dog whose ready acceptance of change made him more hardy than most of his kind. Even amongst his wild brothers there were few that could match him for strength and endurance. He had a master who loved him. Whatever discomfort that master suffered, Petrus himself endured with a measure of stoicism. In the seasons that lay ahead, this was to stand him in good stead.

Thus he emerged from the tribulation of the storm little ruffled in temperament but with greater knowledge of the hazards that could be expected in the nomadic life he lived with his master.

It was no lush world that followed the subsidence of the flood water in the Jordan Valley. Silt covered much of what had been grassland, and since it was salted from the overflow of water from the Dead Sea, the sheep Saul had brought into the valley for good grazing found the pasture hard and bitter to the tongue. As a result their progress toward full maturity was much slower than Saul had expected.

However, as the sun dried up the sodden land, a new growth appeared where before there had been a thick layer of sand and mud. The grass, fresh and green, tasted exceptionally sweet to the ewes that grazed upon it, and it was not long before there was a distinct improvement in the condition of his flock. Soon, then, the shepherd was confidently expecting the first of his lambs.

By this time the sheep were well up the Jordan Valley where a tributary that rose below Shechem flowed down to the main stream, and hereabout followed a course to the Dead Sea that lay a full 1290 feet below the level of the ocean.

The hot and sulphurous salt springs added to the humid atmosphere. For the most part, however, the days were tolerable, and Saul and Petrus, now in a well-situated camping site, were able to relax a while before the long hours with the flock would be necessary with the coming of the first lambs.

When it became too hot for ordinary comfort, Saul and the dog withdrew to one or other of the limestone caves that were a special feature of the mountain structure that reared above them and spread in a northerly direction to the low country of Philistia.

Petrus loved the coolness of the caves and the peculiar scents associated with them. He found once again, as in his puppyhood on the Hill of Hebron, that the only comforting things about life were its smells and the distant glimpse of sunlight through the opening in the rock.

It was a harking back to those days beneath the cairn when, with his quarrelsome sisters, he had lain waiting for his mother to return. The constant change of light and shade he experienced now was much the same as the change he had witnessed then. So, too, was the trickle of wind that came blowing up from the salt marshes by the river. The very sound it made was the same as that which, in the dim recesses of his mind, he associated with the murmuring outside the cairn where he had rested with his nose on his paws, listening intently for a footfall outside.

The main difference now, however, was the man scent in the cave which he had long grown to love and trust. There was no strangeness about that which he could not understand, no spasm of fear.

With this knowledge comforting him, he was able to lie full length at the feet of Saul, his nose within an inch or two of the sandals. His senses in such moments were mainly concerned with smell, touch and hearing. Thus, even while he dozed, he still received impressions of all that went on, either in the cave or without.

So until lambing time was the pattern of hours as spent by Saul and his dog Petrus.

When at last the ewes began to bring forth their young, both Saul and Petrus were kept busy. Not only were they with the sheep during the sunlit hours of every day, but also were amongst them during the long night watches when the air grew cold and the stars shone like bright lamps lit in a far-off country that knew neither boundaries nor time.

Saul, through a lifetime of experience with sheep, knew exactly when a ewe might be expected to lamb. Even if he were taking a short respite from his vigil, he would be on the alert at the right moment, and there would be Petrus approaching to warn him that a lamb was about to be born.

His lantern, during such nights, was never without its full quota of oil, burning clearly to guide him over the many obstacles that might limit his activities.

So constant was he, and so patient with the ewes, that never a lamb did he lose, nor yet a ewe, no matter how difficult her time had been.

Yet, toward the end of the lambing, there was one small creature he might have lost, but for Petrus. It was a black lamb which he was rearing by hand because its mother refused to attend to its wants. Somehow or other it succeeded in breaking free of its tether and vanished.

Saul had discovered that the lamb was missing on his return from an early morning patrol of the flock. Although the day promised to be hot like those that had gone before, as yet, in the half-declared light of dawn, it was quite chilly. The shepherd threw more fuel on his fire, and then prepared himself a meal of toasted bread and meat.

Suddenly, for no better reason than that it seemed very quiet, he glanced around for the black lamb that was usually clamoring to be fed with goat's milk at this hour. It was then he discovered it was missing, and when he went to examine the tether he found that the hide thong that had been about the animal's neck had come apart.

Without further consideration for his own needs, Saul cast around anxiously, seeking some sign of the lamb. As daylight was now strongly entrenched over the valley he could see a great distance, but nowhere amongst the sheep could he glimpse the one he sought.

He then started to search along the edge of the cliffs supporting the mountain plateau. While there were numerous grassy hollows where a stray sheep might be expected to lie concealed, he discovered no black lamb.

Perhaps while he had been away amongst the sheep, some wild beast had come down off the mountain and taken the defenseless lamb.

The herdsman hurried back to the spot where the lamb had been tethered. There was nothing likely to suggest that a wild dog or boar had been anywhere near. The evidence, as far as Saul could determine, lay in the thong which had apparently broken at a weak point, giving the lamb its freedom.

That morning Saul ate his breakfast sorrowfully. He hated losing a living thing that might, at that very moment, be lying hurt in some unsuspected place.

Later, after Petrus, following his usual morning roundup of scattered members of the flock, had eaten his meal which Saul always prepared at the same time as he did his own, the shepherd could no longer restrain his anxiety.

While he was trying to think how best to set about further search, he noticed Petrus sniffing the ground where the animal had been tethered.

Saul jumped to his feet and, hastening forward, encouraged the dog in his casting about. Petrus moved off at a slow pace, making for the deep frown of the cliffs and the dark entrance to a cave which, till then, Saul had scarcely noticed.

Saul hurried back to the tent for his lantern, and kindling it he followed Petrus, who had entered the yawning mouth of the cave.

The shepherd pressed forward, the glow from the lantern casting an eerie light amidst the crevices and corners in the cave. Stalactites, like curiously shaped icicles, hung from the roof of the immense cavern. Some had even formed into twisted pillars of limestone, in places dividing the cave into small apartments. These at a remote period had been the dwelling places of those who, having escaped from the terrors of fire brought down from heaven upon the Cities of the Plain, had lived like hermits until starvation had overtaken them and they had died.

Saul's vision was limited because of the dimness of the light he carried. He could not see Petrus at all, but heard him sniffing his way along what had become little more than a narrowing corridor.

There was a damp coldness in the atmosphere, and the silence was now broken by the constant dripping of water from the roof. Fear gripped the herdsman's heart. He wondered how much longer he dared continue, pressing on into the very bowels of the mountain.

Suddenly he heard Petrus whining anxiously.

Saul quickened his steps, holding the lantern high above his head. He stumbled for an instant, his feet having kicked against an object that had rolled away under the impact.

He paused to see what it was, and was horrified to glimpse a grinning skull. Not far from it was a heap of bones, glimmering white in the light of the lantern. While he was once more aware of fear, before he could register any reaction to it, Petrus gave a short bark which came muffled through the gloom. Guided by it, the shepherd crept forward, and there, in a deep hollow, crouched the dog and the black lamb.

Saul lay on his stomach, and managed to gather the lamb into his arms. Then, with a word of affection for Petrus, he took up the lantern, and rising to his feet started to lead the way back to the outer world.

He was comforted and his fears dispelled by the feel of the lamb in the crook of his arm. Moreover, he knew that Petrus was hard at his heels, and the way therefore did not seem so long as he had supposed it might be.

Soon the gray half-light of the outside world started to filter in through the entrance to the cavern. The stalactites, now glimpsed against the opaque screen of diffused sunshine, appeared grotesque and frightening. Some were like spears suspended from the roof, others like blunted fingers groping downward.

Saul was truly thankful when at last he was in the most lofty part of the cave and saw the opening scarcely more than twenty feet away.

The glare of the sunlight outside dazzled his eyes. The freshness of the air after the cold atmosphere of the cavern was like strong wine in his lungs. He paused for a few seconds to accustom himself to it, aware of Petrus sitting on his haunches beside him, looking up at him with eyes that were eloquent with expression.

He smiled down at the dog, and murmured his name with infinite tenderness in his voice. Saul then proceeded toward the tent, rejoicing within himself because, as in the case of the child Martha, what had been lost was found again. Once more it was the dog Petrus that had brought it about.

And it was as though a voice rising up within him said: 'Take heed always to the wisdom of animals, and fortunate shalt thou be in the fields and in all thy labors. Thou shalt see the increase of thy kine, and the flocks of thy sheep, and know happiness all thy days . . .' Saul wondered if, by chance, he was not hearing the voice of God Himself.

Thinking thus, Saul sat for a long time by his campfire, with the black lamb asleep in his arms and Petrus dozing at his feet. He was, in that hour, filled with a contentment he had not known for many days.

15: The Hour of the Prophet

SOON THE time came for Saul to leave the Jordan Valley. He made a careful examination of the flock and found to his great delight that, without exception, the sheep were lusty and strong and well able to take the journey to the annual market in Jerusalem.

The shepherd broke camp on a morning that was particularly fine and bright. Petrus, anxious to get the flock on the move, kept running backward and forward, and the sheep were soon aware that they were to leave the pasturelands of the Jordan. The dog's repeated movements around them were all too familiar.

It was to be no easy journey to reach Jerusalem. First there was a long trek up into the more remote fastnesses of the Jordan Valley, and then an arduous climb up to the great central mountain escarpment by a track that was rough and winding for more than two-thirds of the way.

Saul, who had made the journey many times before, had no doubt but that it would be safely accomplished. Petrus, with his almost uncanny knowledge of herding, would see to it that the sheep did not wander. For the rest, it was just a continuous plodding up and on — a time, usually, for contemplation. Saul, who was not concerned with haste, liked a journey such as this, for it could be leisurely, and give him freedom for thought. Many a time on a similar trek, he had communed with himself, and finding much amiss, had discovered in the solitudes a quietness that enabled him to put right that which troubled him.

He therefore set off for Jerusalem with confidence, Petrus rounding up the sheep immediately he received his master's commands. Soon the grazing place was deserted. Saul and his flock were traveling up the long valley that, mile by mile, grew more desolate, with the mountain range, deeply scored by ravines, closing in from the north.

It took the shepherd all of four days to traverse the valley and reach the outskirts of Jericho near the junction of a river that flowed into the Jordan from the heights of Moab Gilead. He chose a quiet and sheltered place to set up a temporary camp, where a group of olive trees, long past their flowering, cast melancholy shadows upon the ground and upon the river.

The grazing was good, and the sheep soon scattered under the watchful eye of Petrus.

As night came down, Saul lay full length by the river, his dog at his side. It was warm and pleasant, with the stars once again bright in a cloudless sky, and the only sound, the slow purling of the river. There were moments when Saul, gazing up at the stars, thought he saw a solitary star falling down the unbroken arc of the sky. There were other moments when, with his eyes closed, he heard the voice of the river rising and falling, never in joy, it seemed, but always in a low keening like a lost soul in sorrow.

Saul found his mind slipping back along the years he had known, and wondered if, of all people, he had not had his fair share of sorrow. He struggled to remember the things that had hurt him, but could not recall any of them. There was, somehow, always something else he remembered, a gleam of sunlight on the crest of a breaking wave, a glow of color on a leaf recently born. Even when he tried to think how often folk had spoken harshly to him, there was something else that took the sting away — a smile from a child, the look from a lamb that had lost its mother, the piping voice of a bird.

The shepherd stirred, wondering if perhaps the river was not singing its age-old story of timeless legend, in which sorrow and joy ran hand in hand, with a mournful note, maybe, to enhance the beauty that always lies at the river's end.

Saul sat up, and as he did so, his hand encountered the soft head of Petrus, who rolled over onto his back in play.

The old man sensed then that sorrow was a mere condition of the mind. One had only to stand up and face it as one would Mount Sinai, and he would find himself face to face with God!

That night, under the bright stars, Saul the shepherd and his dog lay side by side in peace. The voice of the river was no more the voice of sorrow, but of joy, eternal, and always ahead.

Jerusalem on this occasion of Saul's visit was thronged with people. There were Jews, Philistines and Ethiopians, all jostling one with the other. Men from the Far East were there too, with silks and spices to sell; others with ornaments from Egypt.

These, however, were not all. Apart from the annual market, which was of special significance throughout Judaea, there had come into the city one who called himself a prophet. He spoke in a loud voice of the trials and tribulations of the Jews, and said that all this was because they had submitted to the Roman conquerors without insisting on their just rights as citizens.

There was with him a gathering of young people, and some verging on to full manhood. All were of a type to be influenced by one with a persuasive tongue. Sprinkled amongst them were those who were little better than thieves and who, for the most part, sought to exploit to their own advantages the feeling of unrest evoked by the so-called prophet's fiery utterances.

Saul, heedless of these events which were soon to involve him, attended the market place and sold his flock to a rich man who possessed a vineyard and good grazing at Emmaus. All morning, the bidding for cattle and sheep, and even slaves, had been brisk. The rich man's stewards went amongst the shepherds and cattlemen, taking stock of what they had to offer, and trying to come to what they considered was a just and fair bargain. One such steward, coming to Saul, cast an appraising eye over his sheep and found them more than usually favorable. He noted their excellent condition despite the journey they had made, and saw that the season's lambs were not only well developed but in good fleece.

He accordingly hurried away to his master and suggested that he should come to the market place and examine the flock himself.

This the rich man did, and as a result Saul was well re-warded for his patience and hard work. He received a very good price for the entire flock, and prepared to leave the market place with his purse heavy with silver pieces. More-over, this time, as distinct from other occasions when he had disposed of his flock, he was not sore at heart. He was given to understand that the rich man intended to retain the flock and put it to graze on his choicest pastures at Emmaus. With it, he hoped, in the not-too-distant future, to build up one of the best and largest flocks of sheep in that part of the coun-try.

Two blind men, sitting side by side in the market place, had been listening to the bargaining and perceived that Saul had been exceedingly well paid for the sheep. As the shep-herd hastened from the overcrowded square, one of them stumbled after him, and catching hold of his robe called loudly for alms.

Saul had ever been the friend of the poor and afflicted, and as was his habit, gave what he considered a generous offer-ing.

The blind man, unfortunately, was an unscrupulous and exacting individual. He was also, in some ways, a student of human nature, knowing that most men were sensitive when reviled in public.

He therefore proceeded to put his knowledge to his own advantage, and complained at the uncharitable ways of those who having struck a good bargain with the rich man from Emmaus, were yet meager in their alms. More than this, he constantly referred to the amount the shepherd had received by the sale he had made.

Greatly disconcerted by this unexpected turn of events, Saul, with Petrus close beside him, made to hurry away and thus escape the blind man's objectionable remarks.

The fellow, quite undaunted by his affliction, continued to harry him. Many of the passers-by, listening to the blind man, quietly marked out Saul as a man of wealth. Among them were three men from Ephraim who were known as the consorts of thieves and evildoers. They were ill-clad in robes that were ragged and soiled. Hearing the blind man's repeated comments, they contrived to keep the old herdsman in sight for the rest of the day.

Despite the good fortune that had attended his bargaining at the market that morning, Saul found it impossible to obtain shelter in Jerusalem for the night. Having eventually evaded the blind man, he had tramped from place to place; every inn was full, and nobody wished to give him lodging with a dog.

Finally, after a rest, Saul decided to leave the city and set off on the road to Jericho. From thence, he planned to travel back along the Jordan Valley to Nain. Perhaps this time, he would come to an arrangement with Naomi and Jacob, and dwell with them for the remainder of his life.

Perhaps, after all, there was something in what Naomi used to say, and that he was indeed too old for the arduous task of herding sheep. The more he considered it, the more he had to acknowledge that he most certainly grew tired more quickly these days. Even so, he was not altogether disconcerted at the discovery. It was almost as though the knowledge had been deep-seated within him for many days.

It was approaching evening when soldiers, led by a burly

centurion, apprehended the prophet, and sent his followers shouting and running through the narrow streets.

Saul was overtaken by some of them as he took the road to Bethany. They fled, jeering and cursing, a motley crowd that only a man with a grievance could muster about him. Not a few carried cudgels and sticks which they waved in the air. Others merely ran, with their faces partially hidden in their robes so as not to be recognized by the soldiers who were in pursuit.

With them came the three men who were known to be the intimate associates of thieves. Beholding Saul and his dog on the road, they fell back from the others and, escaping the pursuing soldiers by hiding in an olive grove, took to the road again when the way was clear.

Meanwhile, Saul, having kept aloof from the fleeing mob and the soldiers, pressed on into the gathering evening light, little knowing that the three men were following less than five hundred paces in the rear.

The shepherd was weary. His footfalls were slow and labored; he made no attempt to hurry. He just took his time, deciding to set up his tent by the wayside, and there rest the night.

He chose a spot where a ditch and a high bank offered him protection from the chill night wind that often blew across this high mountain plateau. With Petrus keenly alert, watching everything he did, Saul set up his small camp and made a fire. He then prepared his meal, and within a short while was ready for sleep.

One or two folk late returning from Jerusalem, passed along the road, with their asses burdened down with wares from the market. Except for these, there seemed nobody abroad. The rabble had departed, and it was silent.

Saul soon slept soundly, with Petrus snug against his back.

16: One Who Fell by the Wayside

THE LAST wisps of smoke from Saul's campfire curled up into the air. As it went eddying away on a sharp race of wind, the fire itself flickered for the last time and died in its ashes. The silence remained unbroken. So clear was the night that the distant horizon was etched in wavering lines against the sky. A group of very bright stars lay low down where the humped summit of Mount Hebron broke the eastern horizon. The road from Jerusalem was clearly defined throughout most of its length from the city, running over the plateau like a piece of string, pulled taut, and unwinding.

It wanted but another hour or so and the night would be gone. The tent set up beside the ditch showed as a dark shadow against the stark uprising of the hedge behind it with no glow of firelight or smoke anywhere.

At the very hour when the night was at its quietest, the first of the three men, bent on robbing the old shepherd, crept from the place where he and his two companions had been in hiding. He paused for a moment, staring into the gloom as if to accustom his eyes to the change of scene. He saw the white surface of the road glimmering before him, and alongside it, at a distance of no more than two hundred paces, the dark smudge of the herdsman's tent. He nodded

his head with satisfaction, and called to his friends very
quietly.

'Now is the time,' he said.

One by one they crept forward from the hollow where
they had been resting. They stood for a few seconds close
together, discussing how best to carry out the contemplated
robbery without rousing the shepherd's dog.

The first man said it could not be done.

'We must remember,' said he, 'that yonder dog has been
trained to the herding of sheep. I've heard tell of him from
another shepherd who dwells in Gath.'

One of the others disappeared for a few minutes, and
when he returned, he carried three heavy staves. There was
a grim, vicious look on his face as he distributed the staves.

'It is best to be prepared,' he said. 'If so be it we cannot
get what we seek without trouble from the old man and his
dog, we shall have to hide all trace of our visit, aye, and even
of his presence here in this place.'

His companions, thinking of their own safety, were in
agreement with him.

Soon afterward, the three thieves crept forward, treading
quietly and choosing the darkest side of the road which was
close to the hedge. Each man gripped his stave; callous and
without qualm about its use.

Petrus, who was sleeping soundly, awakened immediately
the flap of the tent was pulled apart. He half raised his head,
his nostrils widely flared, his body trembling with nervous
anticipation. He had heard no sound, having awakened by
an instinctive impulse that warned him of danger.

There was then that curious pause so often evident in the
ives of men and animals — a pause tense with uncertainty
ind at the same time subtly aware of what the next second
vas likely to bring forth.

Petrus was an animal possessed of a mental vision strong
:nough to embrace instantly what was taking place. The
growl in his throat roused the old man immediately.

A second later, the dog had leaped at the distorted shadow
hat, crouching forward, sought to peer into the gloom of
he tent. His outthrust paws encountered the soft, yielding
ihape of one of the thieves who, with a cry, fell backward.

There was an answering shout. As Petrus, now fully alive
:o the danger that threatened his master, prepared to attack
:he remaining two shapes towering over him, he was
knocked breathless by a blow that nigh broke his ribs.

Even as he rolled over, other, more savage blows, were
iimed at him.

Just when he could scarcely see for pain, he heard his
master cry out in agony. He struggled to his feet, avoiding
yet another blow. He was, however, feeling very sick. Even
so, he still possessed reserves of vitality. Between sharp
spasms of pain, power gathered in his hind legs, and as the
:hief above him swung his staff for yet another crushing
blow upon his body, Petrus was at him, his jaws sinking
deeply into the fleshy part of the fellow's right arm.

The man let out a sharp yell. One of the other shadows
dimly discerned by Petrus, rushed from a point close to the
:ent. Heavier and stronger blows fell upon the dog's body
until he sank back exhausted and unconscious. Even then,

he was kicked until the fellow seemed wearied by his own
brutality and could scarcely raise either arms or legs to con
tinue with the assault.

There was no further outcry from the shepherd. Saul lay
in a heap, his body badly bruised and blood issuing from hi
lips. He still breathed, but he was clearly near death.

None of the thieves heeded him, however. One, stil
clutching his arm where Petrus had bitten deeply, reviled
both the shepherd and his dog. He only hoped that his com
panion had killed the animal, but he was much too con
cerned with his own condition to go and make sure. Of the
three, he was the most superstitious. They had better ge
clear of this place.

He began to bind up his arm with a piece of dirty linen
As he did so, the thief, who had so brutally assaulted the
shepherd, peered out through the opening of the tent, whis
pering that they had better hasten with their looting and be
off before dawn came.

The wounded man agreed vigorously. 'We must surely
be well away from this place before the sun comes up,' he said
hoarsely.

No word had he for the man who lay scarcely breathing
in the tent. His only thought was to plunder the camp and
leave little or no trace of their visit. He could attend more
thoroughly to his arm when he and his companions were
well out in the hills.

The other two were going through the shepherd's belong
ings with such care as only thieves know. They had soon
discovered Saul's purse, still well filled with silver pieces, and

also one or two other items which they deemed might be of value.

At last, they realized that, for their own safety, they had better dismantle the tent itself and take all the herdsman's belongings with them.

They proceeded without delay to sort out the various items of supplies and to package them in a manner easy for carrying. Not many minutes later, they hauled the old shepherd into the open, and after going through his robes for any further trinkets likely to possess a market value, they threw his body into the ditch regardless of whether he was alive or dead. They flung Petrus alongside his master, finally scattering over them dried grass and debris.

They dismantled the tent and then proceeded with the utmost care to obliterate all possible traces of their crimes. In this, all three worked methodically, for they did not wish the soldiers to be sent out after them — not that the Roman conqueror was likely to be much concerned with the fate of an old itinerant shepherd and his dog.

It was best to avoid any contact with the ruling authority, particularly since all three were known throughout the whole of Judaea and Samaria as thieves and the consorts of evildoers.

By now, the night was growing old, its last hour having come. A chill wind came in from off the distant sea. It came searching over the mountain plateau like invisible fingers writing in the brightening sky the history of what had taken place under the cover of darkness.

The three thieves, growing moment by moment more

apprehensive, shivered a little as they continued with their grim task, but before the first light of day appeared in the east, they had departed from the scene of their crimes, taking with them the tent and the remainder of Saul's property.

Only the gray ash of what had once been a campfire showed where a man had rested only to fall among thieves who had stripped him of his goods and left him for dead, with his dog alongside him.

Of this man, it was later to be said:

'A certain man went down from Jerusalem to Jericho, and fell among thieves, which stripped him of his raiment, and wounded him, and departed, leaving him half dead.'

17: He Who Was the Good Samaritan

DAWN BROKE and the east was a wide shimmering stretch of amber light that spilled down upon the great central mountain mass of Judaea until not a shadow remained, and darkness was driven, like a fugitive, from the hills and the valleys. Low down in the very van of the sunrise, the morning star still shone pale and wan like a lamp failing for lack of oil.

As the star finally flickered and died, there was a movement from the ditch where, in the evening, a camp had been set up. A little later, there was the sound of scrabbling on the earth and stones, accompanied by the broken whines of an animal in pain.

Then slowly, panting with great distress, Petrus, the sheepherding dog of Saul, managed to haul himself out of the depression, only to fall weak and trembling upon the surface of the road.

He lay for some minutes motionless, unable to raise his head to bark. His body was filled with unending pain.

After what seemed an eternity to the dog, Petrus managed to pull himself out of the great darkness that, over and over again, welled up and threatened to engulf him for the last time. His jaws lolled open and he began to pant once more. His distress was still acute, and his eyes, when he opened them, were glazed and bloodshot.

The day was, by this time, fully declared, with tattered banners of crimson fluttering over what was the distant hump of Mount Hebron.

As the dog continued the great struggle to bring movement back into his limbs, he turned his head away from the harsh light of the risen sun as if he could not bear the brightness. Then still panting, and breathing spasmodically, he proceeded to drag himself back to the ditch where his master lay.

It was as much as he could do to reach it, short though the distance was, and after struggling inch by inch, all he could do was lie with his head over the edge of the ditch. He was, for the time being, completely done for; he could move no farther.

One broken whine came from him as he sought to raise himself a little to look into his master's face. Then his head went down limply, and he lay with his muzzle overhanging the depression, oblivious to further pain, and scarcely conscious.

At the third hour after sunrise, there passed along the road to Jerusalem one who was a priest of the people. He rode an ass that, apart from the man himself, was well burdened with heavy bundles. The animal shied abruptly when he came to that part of the road where Petrus lay.

The priest had been idly dreaming, and was rudely awakened when the ass made a jump that took him some yards to the other side of the highway.

With a gasp of annoyance, the man dismounted and crossed over to examine the dog. He then glanced into the ditch and saw Saul.

He was badly shaken at the sight that met his eyes. He perceived that this was the work of thieves, and not wishing to become involved in any way with the authorities in Jerusalem, the priest, without ascertaining whether or not the shepherd was alive, hastily remounted his ass and passed by on the other side of the road.

About the fourth hour after sunrise, another chanced to pass along the highway, also traveling toward Jerusalem. This man, considered of some importance among his brethren, saw only the body of the dog, and not wishing to waste time on a mere animal, pressed on without so much as a backward glance.

So Petrus lay for another hour or so. It had become very hot indeed. No cloud in the sky tempered the heat at midday, no shade from the hedge offered respite to man or dog.

Then, coming up from out of Jericho, was another man, also riding an ass. He had with him a pack animal in addition to the creature he rode, and as he came to the spot where the dog lay, a cry of compassion broke from his lips.

Petrus had once again succeeded in struggling out of his sickness and pain, and was trying to rise as the Good Samaritan hastened in his direction.

The dog turned his head with difficulty, looking up into the stranger's face. He sensed at once, despite the weakness in him, that here was no robber to do further harm to his master and himself. As if to show the man he understood, he attempted to wave his tail.

'Fear not,' a voice said gently, and a hand moved over the animal's bruised body tenderly.

The man then glimpsed the body of Saul still unconscious in the ditch.

Leaving the dog, he bent over the depression, and gently drew the body out, laying it upon his own outer raiment which he had spread out upon the rough surface of the road.

He saw at once that Saul's condition was serious. The old shepherd had been most sorely treated. Taking some oil of olives from his supplies, and tearing up a strip of fine linen, he proceeded to cleanse the herdsman's wounds. He then gave him some strong wine in an effort to revive him.

After a little while, Saul showed some sign of recovering, and the stranger made him as comfortable as was possible, then he turned his attention to Petrus.

Examining the dog as carefully as he had the animal's master, he found no bones broken, but the dog's body was badly bruised, and there were several deep cuts on the flanks which required immediate attention.

As he had done with the dog's master, so now he did to Petrus, rubbing oil into his body and bathing the cuts to ease the soreness.

It was late in the afternoon before Petrus had regained sufficient strength to stand and walk about. Saul, while conscious, was still very ill indeed.

The stranger, perceiving that it would be best to get the old man to the city as quickly as possible, managed after much effort to set the shepherd up on one of the asses. Then after ensuring as best he could that Saul did not fall from the creature's back, he started off for Jerusalem. Petrus followed slowly and painfully in the rear, dragging his hind legs like one sick with a plague.

Never in his life before had the stranger known the way into the city to be so long and troublesome. More than once he had to support the shepherd. Most of the time, he had to keep up a steady flow of conversation to keep the old man alert lest he lapse again into unconsciousness and so fall from the ass.

At last Jerusalem came into sight. There were few people in the narrow streets, for the hour was late. Those that were about were much too concerned with their own affairs to give more than a casual glance at the stranger and Saul. The few that did saw nothing amiss save that the dog stumbled as he walked, and was panting heavily.

It was no easy matter to get accommodation for the shepherd, but after much persuasion on the part of the stranger, Saul was at last taken into an inn. Petrus was put into an adjoining stable with the traveler's two asses.

For the whole of the night, the man sat at the bedside of Saul, ministering to his wants and doing what he could to ease the herdsman's suffering. It was clear that Saul was gravely ill. His breathing was labored and he was in a high fever. Toward midnight, he became delirious and constantly asked for the dog.

Despite the innkeeper's disgust at having an animal in the dwelling, Petrus was finally brought into his master's room where he remained until morning.

With another day, the Good Samaritan was faced with a further problem. He had a far journey to make, and could not tarry overlong in Jerusalem.

As soon as it was light, he again attended to Saul's wounds and also to those of Petrus. He then prepared food for both, and was disconcerted when he found that the shepherd was unable to partake of even a little goat's milk. While the old man was no longer delirious, he was much weaker, his body still torn with pain.

The traveler consulted with the innkeeper and paid him for the night's lodging. He then gave his host a further sum, saying: 'Take care of the old man and his dog. Whatsoever thou spendest over and above this amount, when I come again I will repay thee.'

The innkeeper was greatly moved by such unexpected generosity. Never before could he remember such a thing being done. He therefore promised to do as the traveler asked, and even went so far as to permit Petrus to remain in the sick man's room.

Another night came — another day. On the third day, Saul the shepherd, the last surviving son of Daniel, the legendary herdsman of Arimathaea, died of his wounds.

18: The Cry of the Forlorn Heart

WHILE HE had been kind to Petrus because of his devotion to Saul, the innkeeper still regarded him as something only to be tolerated for a short period. The man had not thought that the shepherd would ultimately die of his wounds, despite his obvious weakness. His own experience with these itinerant herdsmen had shown him that they were as tough as the life they lived. He had not understood exactly how old Saul was, nor how sorely he had been treated by the thieves.

The dog, however, had a foreboding of what was to happen. All that last night, he lay at the foot of the rough couch that made up his master's bed. His own wounds were healing miraculously, and the sickness was entirely gone from his body. There was, moreover, a new strength springing up in him that was not entirely due to his previous good condition. It was as though, with the approaching end of his life with Saul, new forces were giving him a different strength of will and courage to face a world that, for one such as he, alone and masterless, might prove even more difficult and hostile.

Meanwhile, Petrus lay at the foot of his master's couch, watching and waiting. That end of which he was so sensitively aware came with the weakened voice of his master saying: 'Petrus . . . Petrus . . . Petrus . . .'

Just three times the utterance of the name the old man had grown so much to love, and then, as a last comfort, the feel beneath his dying fingers of fur that was warm and soft to the touch.

As Petrus gazed into his master's graying face, he knew that no more would Saul speak to him. The end had indeed come!

The dog was grieving silently when the innkeeper came, and the man, seeing the manner of thing that had taken place, put a leather thong about the animal's neck and took him out to the stable to await the return of the stranger who the man felt would put in an appearance with a few days.

Petrus went quietly and without a backward glance at that which had not moved during the hours he had lain watching. He sensed, rather than understood, that never more would he behold the man he had known as master and friend.

The dog continued to grieve as he lay on a heap of straw in the stable which now housed some oxen and a very morose ass. There was, nevertheless, a growing consciousness that, sooner or later, he would have to leave the stable and go forth to face his future.

Petrus had no way of knowing what stirred in him beyond the grief he felt at the loss of Saul. He only knew that as the long hours slipped by, taking him farther and farther away from that last utterance of Saul, there was new strength welling up in him. It brought a subtle awareness of the new vitality that lay in his fast-healing limbs, and the new determination beating in his heart.

The ass watched him sullenly, then continued with his

munching of hay. Likewise the oxen, after they had become used to the dog's presence amongst them, forgot him and also ate unceasingly, the rhythmic movement of their jaws bringing Petrus finally to the quietness of sleep.

The innkeeper came at nightfall and brought the dog food to eat and fresh water in an earthenware pot. He looked down at the dog and paused for a moment, wondering. There was a curious change in the animal. The pain of grief still lay deep in the brown eyes that looked up at him, but the body was no longer drawn in pain but appeared vigorous like an animal in the pride of health. The wounds on his flanks had almost vanished. More than that, the moment Petrus sniffed the food, he rose and began to eat.

A strange thought came to the innkeeper as he watched. The dog was suddenly like a creature that had been reborn and upon whom the hand of a new destiny lay lightly, but nevertheless unmistakably.

It seemed to the man that the dog was merely awaiting the hour when he must set off to journey to the place where his fulfilment awaited him.

The innkeeper was truly puzzled. He shook his head, then, with the burial of the dog's master on his mind, turned to hasten away. At the entrance to the stable, he paused again and looked back at the animal.

Petrus returned the look unflinchingly.

The innkeeper came to an abrupt decision.

'When I've seen to the burial of his old master, I'll return and make him my own dog,' he said to himself.

His previous dislike of dogs and the words of scorn he had ofttimes used in connection with them, were forgotten in the new wonder that was springing up in him at sight of the nobility in the animal who had come to the inn half dead and who was now so completely changed.

He hurried back to the inn and the sorry task that awaited him, anxious now to get everything done so that he could return to the dog.

Saul was buried in one of the old caves used for the purpose. When it was quite dark, the old herdsman's body, wrapped in linen and spices, was put away under the flickering glow of torchlight.

The cave was one used for malefactors and the like, but the innkeeper, remembering how he had been paid by the stranger who had brought the old man to the inn, saw to it that the shepherd was put apart from the others. The crevasse he chose was set in the eastern part of the cave, and was quite isolated from the more frequently used burial places.

Having seen the shepherd thus laid in his last resting place, the innkeeper signified to those who had come with him that there was nothing more to be done.

He suddenly found himself thinking that it was as natural for a man to die as it was for a babe to be born, and that between the two was all the joy and laughter that life gives so lavishly. The man felt that, somehow, Saul had indeed savored the pleasant side of life as he had the sorrowful. Once again came the thought of Petrus who had been the herdsman's constant companion.

The innkeeper knew then without doubting that Saul had, by reason of his association with the dog, been among the most favored of men. He wondered no more and came away from the scene of the burial after the sealing stone had been rolled into place.

When, however, he came again to the stable, Petrus had gone, having bitten through the leather thong that, secured by a staple, had held him captive. Neither he, nor anybody else in Jerusalem, was to see the dog again for many days.

Jerusalem, after darkness had fallen, was a place of strange shadows, sounds and smells. Voices were muffled and almost disembodied; pariah dogs haunted the alleys between the gaunt, misshapen dwellings.

As Petrus crawled out of the stable, scratching his way through a broken part of the mud wall, he discerned the distant waving of lights, little knowing that it was caused by the torches of those who were carrying his late master's body to the cave for burial.

The dog paused but a few seconds, staring up at the inn. Since there was no sign of life in it, and he sensed that his master was no longer there, he turned disconsolately away. He took the road that led through the city to the distant mountain plateau where he and Saul had encountered the thieves. He walked aimlessly, having no place now wherein to rest and no master for whom to work.

Once a pariah dog challenged him, the thin, miserable creature coming out from a dark alley where he had been searching amongst the rubbish for something to eat. He bristled at sight of Petrus and bared his teeth in a silent snarl.

Petrus was in no mood either to quarrel or to be friendly. He wanted to be left alone and trotted on slowly and cautiously, fully prepared to defend himself should the other animal make an unexpected move toward him.

The dog, however, suffered Petrus to go on his way, and then, because he was lonely and in need of companionship, proceeded to follow at what he considered was a safe distance. He saw Petrus stop on the outskirts of the city and look back. It was then he took fright. He went running back the way he had come, little knowing that had he pressed on, Petrus, because of a sudden awareness of misery, might have accepted him as a companion.

Petrus remained for a very long time staring at the dark and gloomy city. He was wistful and sad. He sensed that, when he finally left Jerusalem behind, so would he leave the last remaining influence of Saul.

The dog whined. He knew only too well that all that remained of his master lay somewhere in the city. He would not find it out here where the road to Bethany thrust out across the plateau in the direction of the place where disaster had overtaken them both.

Petrus sat back on his haunches. He was very still. It seemed that some strange power held him motionless. Then he whined again. He felt he could hear Saul calling him: 'Petrus . . . Petrus . . . Petrus . . .' But it was only the dead echo of something that no longer existed as a living entity.

Even so, the dog continued to listen, hearing at last not the dead voice but the steady beating of his own heart which was now like thunder in his ears.

Suddenly he stood up, his tail half plumed and his ears erect.

Then, as if in farewell, he gave a loud lament. Thrice did his voice go sounding out into the night, echoing down the dim corridors of the city's mean streets. The dog, who had followed him and who was now back in the winding alleys where the night seemed darkest, heard the sound and paused in his pitiful hunting for food. He would have given a reply but for the fact that a miserable lath of a man came at him from out of the gloom and dealt him a blow with his staff.

Even as he turned and fled from the unexpected attack, so did Petrus, at the city's boundaries, turn and start to lope steadily along the mountain road where, but a few days before, he and Saul had walked together.

A star went falling down the sky as he loped; an owl hooted in the thorn trees beyond the city wall. Then the far-off voice of a soldier shouted that all was well.

After that, no sound at all from the city that was Jerusalem, no light to show that it was inhabited. Nothing — nothing even over the plateau where a road thrust toward Bethany and the far horizon where stars were sinking down to meet the sunrise.

Petrus rested soon after daybreak in the very spot where Saul had set up his last camp. The dog had anxiously sniffed the ground as if hoping against hope that some trace of his master remained. What scent there was scarcely possessed sufficient strength to bring alive the vision of Saul as the dog had last seen him. The only real thing was the gray ash from the campfire. This kindled in the dog's consciousness the memory of smoke twisting upward and the tent that had been set before it.

Then as he lay with his nose on his outstretched paws,

gazing sorrowfully at the ash, one final glimpse he had of Saul. The old herdsman was bending over him, smiling as so often in life he had smiled.

'Go, Petrus,' he seemed to say, 'follow the road and thine own destiny. The end for thee is not yet, nor yet in any known time in the life of man. . . .'

And hearing that voice from the depths of his being, Petrus, the dog that had been the companion of Saul the herdsman, rose and set off once again, walking directly into the sunrise and the new life that lay out beyond the limits of the hills of Judaea.

By the Sabbath, Petrus had come down off the great plateau of the mountains and was on the outskirts of Jericho, where he and Saul had rested on that last journey they both made with the sheep. The sadness in his heart was now less intense. There was something else taking possession of his whole being, and it was behind the great restlessness that urged him to continue traveling on and on.

It was also in the vague probing that made him turn once more to the east and proceed far up the Jordan Valley until he came at last to that place where his mother had met the wild dog.

Like his mother before him, Petrus found that the vast salt marshland adjoining the Dead Sea was not good for either living or hunting. As a result, like her, he grew thin and turned his eyes to the Hill of Hebron that stood a long way off, as bleak and desolate as on that day his mother beheld it. Moreover, he was oppressed by the attention he received from the vultures who dwelt high up in the limestone caves.

Finally there came a day when the dog decided to take to the hills himself. In this he was guided by a sense of self-preservation. Perhaps it was the ghost of the shepherd bitch who told him the way he should go to reach the place where he had been born and which, in a time of need, had given her protection and shelter.

He was a long time journeying up into the hill country before he came to the withering cypress clinging to a rock crevasse high up on the slopes that led to Mount Hebron. It was much cooler there than it had been down in the salt marshlands, and finding the stream of clear water that had once refreshed his mother, Petrus drank deeply and then stretched out to rest.

In his sleeping he was protected by something that was surely out of the ken of other animals, for a boar passed by and saw him not; and when he awakened, there, in a grassy hollow were two brown-furred creatures that fell easy victims to his quick method of attack. Thus, miraculously, his hunger, too, was assuaged.

That night, he slept once again under the withered cypress, but next day, at sunup, he pressed on up the hill and saw, at the twelfth hour, the summit of Mount Hebron rising like a rounded cone. No active memory had he of this place, yet he made instinctively for the cairn. He sniffed amongst the stones and then, by careful manipulation, succeeded in crawling into the very center of the outcrop.

And so Petrus came to the place where he had been born,

and where, with his more unfortunate sisters, he had waited on a moonlit night for the return of the mother who had fed and nourished them.

Something of this came to him as he slept. For one brief impulse of time, like a scene discerned but darkly in a mirror, he beheld the shepherd bitch and those female puppies who had been his companions. Nothing of the distress he had known in this place came back to him in that brief glimpse he had into the past that, like the dream it was, ended within a dream.

Soon, his quiet breathing was that of an animal who slept, sure in the knowledge that no harm could befall him.

Petrus tarried for ten days and nights on Mount Hebron. He then, quite suddenly, departed for the old fig tree and the distant valley of the two rivers.

19: A Wanderer in the Wilderness

THERE IS a wise saying, attributed to the scribes of the East, which states that what is not allotted, no being can reach, and what is allotted, all living creatures will surely find wherever they may be. Actions that have been, control in no mean degree the future.

Such might well have been applied to everything Petrus did, from the very hour of Saul's death. His very orientation, while taking him back to places he was acquainted with, was yet leading him unobtrusively to some greater fulfilment already determined by earlier events. The great cycle of his life was spinning toward its inevitable goal, and nothing that might happen to him could change, by as much as a hand's span, what had been set as his final accomplishment.

Thus as the dog set out on his long and lonely trek across the Hill of Hebron to the ancient fig tree and the valley of the two rivers, he was not so much aware of having made the journey before as he was of following this obscure orientation that was becoming stronger as each day passed.

He trotted the winding trail with an easy assurance, hunting when it was necessary to appease the pangs of hunger, resting and sleeping when these became essential for his well-being.

All the while he was conscious that in due time he would understand more fully the restlessness that was now driving him on, and from mere understanding would come to know what it was he actually sought. Then he would yield more completely to the orientation within him, and journey onward to where fulfilment might be found.

Until that hour of enlightenment, Petrus went questing along the ridge of the escarpment and then down toward Beersheba, coming at last to the old fig tree, no longer barren in age, but green and rich in fruit, and bearing in its branches nests where the birds of the air rested and reared their young.

There, because he no longer feared starvation and death, nor the emptiness of the world without a master, Petrus again made a temporary home amongst the roots of the tree, this time fully conscious of having come to a place he recognized and loved.

More than the place itself, Petrus loved the tree and the shade its foliage gave at high noon, intrigued for the most part by the constant movement of birds passing to and fro, not one of which seemed alarmed because the dog had invaded their sanctuary.

Within a day or so, it seemed as if Petrus had always been there. Indeed, for the dog, in this hour of repose, old memories, not quite strong enough to become actual visions in his consciousness, began to stir in him. Not once, however, did they come fully to life. Thus, no vision had he of Saul bending over him and speaking in well-loved tones, no subtle memory of being lifted up and carried as a lamb down to the camping site in the valley of the two rivers.

Yet surely, in the stillness of the evening hush, he heard, while he slept, the soft tread of a sandaled foot on the turf, and when he awakened, heard what might have been the breath of a sigh that stirred the branches above his head.

So strong was this impression one morning that the dog, on waking, went loping rapidly down the trail, not stopping until he came to the rich pastureland at the foot of the escarpment and beheld, near by, the grove of olive trees where ofttimes, in the heat of the day, Saul had taken his ease, and sometimes dozed.

There was no camp in the valley now, no collection of domestic utensils under the trees. Nor were there any sheep. There was, nevertheless, a whispering in the olives caused by a little breeze that wandered complaining amidst the branches, that to Petrus seemed acutely familiar. He felt that he'd heard it often before and in this same place. What he could not determine was the imagery that would have brought alive the figure of Saul, and himself, very young, lying at his feet.

It was about this time that the first pack of jackals gathered for the hunt. From a long way off, the cry of the leader came winding down from the wastes of the hill country. It was a cry fierce and brutish, yet compelling in its intensity.

Petrus heard it and crouched close under the trees, his ears pressed against his skull. This cry he did understand, and needed no imagery to tell him what it foretold. Even as he crouched as if in fear against it, so did something primitive in his nature respond. The wild dog, his sire, seemed to be with him then, filling his blood with all the restless excitement of the hunt.

By the time of the third and fourth calls, Petrus was making for the desolate hill country and the meeting place of the pack.

Unlike that other occasion when he had answered the call of his wild brothers, he did not hesitate when he came to the old fig tree, but continued to thrust on up the slope with all the eagerness of an animal who was one of them. In this, more than anything else, he felt compelled to travel on by the riotous surging in his blood.

It was almost as though in him, the wild dog who had been his sire was mysteriously brought back from the dead, and exulted in the running of the living animal.

Then Petrus came to a stumbling halt. On the ridge itself, an enormous shadow seemed awaiting him.

Petrus bristled with sudden fear. The wind was coming from the wrong direction, and it was not until the shadow took on a more definite form that Petrus identified it as belonging to a jackal.

The animal was in a somewhat better position that Petrus, standing as he was on high ground. The dog, however, was quick in recovering from the shock he had experienced. With a quick movement, he swung away from the trail he had been following. Then before the jackal could interpret his intentions, he stood facing the creature at the same level.

It was a tense moment. Neither animal was sure what the other might do. Their eyes gleamed.

Walking stiff-legged, Petrus advanced cautiously until there was less than three or four paces separating them.

The jackal's shoulders bristled as he stood rigid and nervous. A decoy from the main pack, he had mistaken the scent of Petrus for an animal suitable for hunting down. He therefore was at a disadvantage, and as his eyes stared into those of the dog, he endeavored to come to some sort of understanding with him. A whimper, almost like that of a dog, rose in his throat.

Petrus was misled by it. As a result, his muscles relaxed, and his head went forward slowly, his nostrils widely spread as he sought to test the musk of the jackal.

The scent was neutral, giving him no indication of the other's attitude toward him. Then the jackal, a natural traitor, sniffed noses with Petrus. Not long afterward having won the dog's trust, both stood shoulder to shoulder, staring away into the night.

It was soon afterward that the call of the pack came to them again, winding in a savage paean from off the heights. The jackal understood. The pack was calling him in with the prey.

He turned and nuzzled Petrus as he would one of his own kind. Following this action of betrayal, he set off, the dog following him. Within a matter of seconds, they were running shoulder to shoulder to where the jackals waited in what was wild boar country.

The trail the two followed led inevitably to the broken ravine, and both searched out the bridge of debris in order to cross to the southern side of the escarpment.

They were much too engrossed with reaching the pack to be aware of the sudden movement of stones beneath their feet, and did not hear the falling away of boulders and scree as they hit the trail already taken by the night hunters.

For once, Petrus was glad of the companionship of another animal, and his running was swift and sure. He seemed eager to outrun the jackal. He panted as the pace quickened, and thrilled to the easy movement of his muscles.

At last both animals were racing neck to neck, the excitement of the race having taken complete possession of the jackal. As a result, he was utterly unaware that he and Petrus were approaching the hummocky ground where the pack was lying in wait.

Maybe the jackal, who had so easily betrayed Petrus, was himself betrayed by the contrary wind currents. Just when he should have delivered the dog up for destruction, the sudden change of wind direction caused him to follow it and thus lead Petrus away from the pack.

Almost immediately he knew what he had done, but there was now no way by which he could retrieve his unfortunate error. With his turning away from the pack, the harm had been done, and he knew that he and Petrus were no longer running for the sheer joy of running, but were racing to save their very lives with an outraged pack in full cry behind them.

In his distress, the jackal looked to Petrus for protection. The dog, almost in understanding, swung away in a wide loop, the jackal following. This movement took them behind a series of hummocks. The dog wound in and out of the broken hillocks, and passed over the arena where his mother had met her death. What, however, had been the sheepherding animal's place of destruction proved to be her son's means of deliverance.

Both Petrus and the jackal had temporarily shaken off their pursuers, and by the maneuver through the hummocks succeeded in hitting once again the main trail leading back to the ravine.

Petrus was now somewhat in the lead. Suddenly a rising chorus of howls in the rear told him that the pack had picked up the trail and was in hot pursuit. This lent greater speed to his racing feet, and the jackal was hard put to keep up with him.

At last the ground began to shelve steeply to the north. Above, the rising cliffs on the main ridge towered in a serrated outline on the night horizon.

The dog thrust away from it, and was soon running along the edge of the ravine seeking the natural cleavage in the escarpment where the rubble bridge led to the northern side.

Petrus encountered the bridge rather more quickly than he had anticipated, and before he knew what was happening, found the debris collapsing beneath his weight. As he slipped and rolled, his paws grappled for support. He felt himself propelled forward, then sideways, with the whole of the scree slope falling away with him.

The jackal shot past him with a howl that echoed eerily up the gully. Then as Petrus slithered to a stop, his body arched over a ledge composed of soft earth, he heard savage cries above him as the hunters, also unable to check themselves, hurtled into the ravine.

Animal after animal swept past Petrus where he lay breathless and bruised. The avalanche continued to rumble and roll, and the earth ledge supporting the dog shook and quaked but, fortunately for him, held firm.

The noise of falling rocks and stones, and the howls of stricken animals continued to resound for some time. Then, save for the falling of just one or two small boulders, it was all over.

As for Petrus, he remained clinging to the ledge, hearing the cries of those animals who, broken and dying, tried in vain to struggle out of the ravine. At last the cries ceased. Nothing moved in the darksome depths of the ravine. Petrus alone had survived the avalanche, and when dawn came he scrambled off the ledge and found a way back to the summit, where he lay exhausted while the new day gathered in beauty over the hills.

Once more he had been wondrously preserved while others had perished!

Some three hours later, he was heading in the direction of Mount Hebron, but did not go to the cairn and the lair. Instead, he swung a little to the southeast, and by nightfall had taken up refuge in a barren field where once Saul and other shepherds had watched over their flocks and a bright star in the east had heralded the birth of One named Jesus.

20: To the Land of Morning Calm

A CURIOUS calmness had taken possession of Petrus the very instant he entered the confines of the field. There was sufficient light in the sky to etch the boundaries of what was little more than a wilderness. He could see tufts of coarse grass upon which Saul's sheep had once eaten with contentment, but now there was hardly anything more than a few clumps of wild tamarisk.

Petrus was tired and soon curled up to sleep beside a boulder that offered some support for his back as he pressed against it. No troubled dreams had he and when he awakened, there was only the light-hearted knowledge that day had come, and with it the beginning of a new life.

It was a beautiful morning that broke over the hills and brought a soft light to the field that had been barren. It was peaceful, too. There was dew upon the grass and upon the tamarisk. More than that, there was dew upon some white blossoms that had certainly not been in the field when Petrus entered it a few hours earlier. They seemed to have bloomed overnight, and grew in wild profusion close to the boulder where the dog had slept.

Then bright in the van of the sunrise glowed the morning star that, instead of becoming pale and wan as the sun came up, gleamed the more clearly. It seemed to hang very low in the sky, reminiscent of that other star that had guided the shepherds to the stable in Bethlehem. When Petrus finally loped out of the field upon the narrow trail where once before he had stood with a sense of guilt in his heart, the star was directly ahead of him.

The dog shook himself and stood panting gently. Then he glanced back at the place where he had rested the night. A bird was singing from somewhere in the field, piping out loud and clear. Even as he gazed over his shoulder, Petrus saw the bird, brightly colored and on the wing. It was a lone bird, flying as once before another bird had flown. This time, however, the bird was not heading toward the west, but winging directly into the east where the morning star flickered and burned low, and the banners of the dawn fluttered tremulously.

Not many minutes later, Petrus was running straight into the sunrise and to Bethlehem.

His running that morning was exceptionally effortless. He knew that he had traveled this very path before, but like all else connected with the past, it was only an instinctive awareness that made the ground feel familiar beneath the press of his running feet. Nothing more! He remembered nothing of the earlier circumstances, but knew the very instant when he was approaching the city of Bethlehem. The smell of the place reached him on the morning breeze, and despite the people who were abroad early because it was a market day, he hastened on, coming at last to a quiet courtyard and a stable, the door of which stood open wide.

The morning was now well advanced, and no longer did

A new day had come

the morning star shine in the east. It had flickered and died as Petrus entered Bethlehem.

Petrus paused. There was nobody about to heed him. The only sound was of laughter coming from the inn itself. His confidence grew, and he walked slowly and soundlessly to the stable where he stood on the threshold, looking in. In the half-light of morning, he saw the eaves of the building slanting upward and away out of sight. There was a lantern, too, hanging from one of the beams, but it was unlighted.

Then the dog saw an ass, standing in a stall munching hay. On either side, oxen were patiently chewing, the rhythmic sound a familiar thing in his ears.

Then in a manger he saw what appeared to be a bundle. The dog went forward slowly, raised himself on his hind legs and sniffed the object. It was merely a bundle of linen, left there by an itinerant herdsman.

Petrus fell back a pace or two, and stood silent and still. His instincts were endeavoring to grapple with something he sensed he should never have forgotten. No memory had he of Saul in that moment, Saul who had raised aloft his crook to chastise him. No memory either of the two shepherds who had also come to this place with Saul. Yet there was surely some vague memory after all stirring within him, a memory so different from all those other memories that, at times, had disturbed him. The association lay in that white bundle set high up in the manger!

The dog moved forward again to investigate. Once more he reared up and sniffed the bundle of linen. Then he paused, his ears erect, his head half turned as he listened.

A weak cry had come to his ears — the cry of a babe . . .

Petrus trembled, his eyes suddenly full of distress for something he still was unable to place.

Again the baby cried out. The cry, however, was from without, and not from within the stable. Then a voice — that of a woman — spoke soothingly.

Petrus turned away from the manger and walked to the stable door, the ass and the oxen watching him curiously. There came to the dog then another of the rare moments when he had an inward glance into something that had a direct association with that which he sought.

He saw a woman with a child in her arms, and a bearded man who was the child's father. All three were in the court-yard, and he had seen somebody like them before.

Then he knew — and remembered! His remembrance, however, was only of the mother and child and the man who had been the child's protector. No other figure came to life in the dog's mind — no likeness of Saul, who had been his beloved master for so many years. There was only the sharp remembrance of the baby, the woman and the man.

And then, even as he remembered, the call came to him — the call to go out and journey forth toward the west, and seek out a place near Mount Tabor and the Sea of Galilee. The very intensity of the call, bringing with it so sharp a sense of orientation that he knew exactly the way he should go, set him quivering with a strange, increasing excitement.

He held his head high and sniffed the atmosphere. All he could smell, unfortunately, were the sour scents of the mean streets, and the more readily understood scents of the ass and oxen back in the stable.

Despite these things, Petrus was not perplexed. As he

loped out into the courtyard and stood for a moment looking at the man and the woman, and the baby the woman held against her breast, again it came to him . . . He stood facing the direction of that call from out of the west sounding so clearly in his ears. It was as if the west wind was speaking to him, telling him to set off at once and not hesitate.

The man and woman were watching him, the woman holding her baby tightly against her as if afraid.

Her husband smiled at her and said, 'Fear not, the dog is harmless. He is lost, and seeking his way back home.' Then, with conviction in his tones, he added, 'Seest thou, I am right. He is off. Perchance, at last, he knows the way he should go.'

Indeed, it was so. Petrus had left the courtyard and stood out in the street. Suddenly he was off in earnest, trotting due west. Out there, way beyond Bethany and Ephraim, beyond even Samaria and the Jordan Valley, was the place he sought — the place he sensed was to be his home. No doubt had he as to the way he should go. The call that had come to him, and the attendant sense of orientation was too strong for error.

He passed swiftly through the streets of Bethlehem, coming out onto the open mountain plateau at a point near Bethany where the road to Jerusalem led past the place where Saul had been attacked and brought to his death. Petrus ignored this road, coming down off the mountains into the Jordan Valley a mile or two west of Jericho.

There he hit the trail he had once taken with Saul and the sheep, and within seven days stood beyond the junction of the two rivers and under the shadow of Mount Gilboa.

The days passed, and Petrus traveled on, mile after mile. He rested but little. It seemed that the fevered singing of the blood in his veins would not allow him respite. When he beheld herdsmen with their flocks, he avoided them, and went slipping by like a shadow, often hiding amongst rocks or in caves until they had gone.

In all this time, he was running direct into the wind. It seemed to blow ceaselessly from the west, coming in at the dog strongly. The touch of it upon his head and shoulders was like that of an invisible hand enticing him on. Only once did Petrus desire to turn about and travel with the wind. The instant he obeyed this urge, the wind ceased to blow, and not until he turned again and faced the west did he feel it coming in at him, again with scents that drew him farther and farther into the west from whence it had come.

By now Petrus was close to Nain, where once he had dwelt with Saul and his sister and her husband. He was even traveling close to the plain where he and the child Martha had withstood the jackals.

He made no deviation, however, but kept straight on until another seven days had come and gone. Then suddenly, one morning, he came out onto a plain where the wind blew completely free, as if from an horizon that possessed no barriers. It was a chill wind, too, and ahead of him the dog saw what appeared to be a wide stretch of water.

Petrus hastened on, following the downward run of a river that finally drained into the lake. By the twelfth hour, he stood on the shores of the Sea of Galilee watching the fishermen tending their nets. The great inland sea, on this day of the dog's first visit, was very quiet and very blue. Two fishing boats were putting out from the shore, the fishermen already preparing to cast their nets. They seemed frail upon the dazzling brightness of the water. A few sea birds tossed and turned, indicating a shoal of fish. Their cries reached the dog who had paused, his tail drooping dejectedly.

For the first time in many days, Petrus was conscious of a great weariness. His feet were blistered and sore, and his flanks grown lean from his constant running.

One of the fishermen mending the nets saw him and, shouting, hurled a stone in his direction.

Petrus slunk away, returning when it was nigh dark. He ate from the catch of fish that had been left on the shore to be collected later.

He slept that night close to the great lake, and not until the stars were fading from the sky and gray day had come over the water did he awaken. He limped off once more to the store of fish and was eating his fill when one of the boats that had been out all night came in.

The fishermen saw him robbing them of their earlier catch, and two of the men, jumping ashore, ran at Petrus with sticks and driftwood.

Petrus was caught unawares. Then another man, coming down to meet the boat, began to assist the fishermen in driving him away. Stones were hurled at him, and the dog was badly cut and bruised before he was able to escape.

Conscious of a growing despair and loneliness, he turned away from the Sea of Galilee, and saw the outline of Mount Tabor rising up directly ahead. Even as his sense of loneliness increased, so did the wind come as an ally to him. This time it blew over him, veered slightly and seemed to tell him to travel with it.

Petrus sniffed the air currents. For one short moment he felt an odd elation welling up in him. Then he started to run, but his feet were much too sore to allow him to outstrip the wind. He nevertheless trotted with it, limping badly when the ground became overrough, crying out when once or twice the blisters between his toes broke in blood.

He was in sorry shape. At last, from sheer weariness and pain, he was forced to lie up in a cave under the cliffs of Mount Tabor. It seemed to the dog that the orientation that had previously guided him onward had deserted him entirely, and he was now completely alone in a very lonely world.

His body shivered as he stretched himself out, his nose on his paws. Until now, his spirit had remained unbroken. As he gave a prolonged sigh, the spirit that had sustained him weakened and temporarily gave up. He sighed once more. Never sure of what he was actually searching for, he only sensed with alarm that he had come a long way without finding any comfort for the growing distress in his mind.

Petrus lay for many hours grieving and filled with a loneliness so great that he turned about and buried his nose in his bushy tail, whimpering loudly. He, who had known for so long the companionship of man, was again beginning to remember what it was like to possess a loving master. The world of the wild was not for him!

That night a full moon came up, flooding the whole of the

plain with gold so that the Sea of Galilee was like a gleaming mirror. A great calm lay over all the world. In the plain where no house was built, no stone laid end upon end, the moonglow added to the quietness of the night. It might well have been the fabled wilderness where no man had trod in anger to make war upon his neighbor.

Petrus came out of the cave and looked about him. He gazed down into the plain, and a little of its calm reached up and gave him comfort. As his nostrils widened to take in the night scents, he felt that he had come out of darkness into a light that was all-absorbing and held a pattern which, if he could but read it, would give him the answer he sought.

Then again, as he stood alone within the shadow of the mountain, gazing down upon the plain and the distant Sea of Galilee, Nature began to rouse in him that miracle of orientation that has ever been the salvation of creatures lost and lonely in the world of the wild.

With the subtle movement of moonglow and shadow, the interpretation he sought seemed to be made clear to him. A small voice seemed to be speaking to him once more in accents he readily understood; and again was it in the wind that had come suddenly to him.

He experienced a desire to travel around the mountain in a northerly direction, and as the last of the night fishermen put out in their boats, the dog obeyed the prompting of the wind and the urge in his heart and, limping, followed what was clearly a much-used trail.

The great calm of the plain remained with him, so that he journeyed without fear.

Night had gone and the sun was well up when Petrus beheld in the distance some herdsmen with their flocks. He was about to hide from them when he saw that he was within sight of a village set somewhat precariously within the grip of the surrounding hills.

Then, because he was so utterly weary, and his feet so blistered and raw, he continued on, and thus came to Nazareth. He sensed, with relief, that his long journey was nigh at an end!

21: The End of the Quest

NAZARETH, built amidst the foothills of Mount Tabor, was a straggling village, the small houses for the most part being set close together on account of the undulating nature of the country. In them dwelt herdsmen and tillers of the fields, also some fishermen who kept their boats on the shores of the Sea of Galilee and who journeyed to their fishing on asses. There were also those who bought and sold and had their small premises of business in Nazareth itself, and two or three swarthy-faced folk from Ptolemais, the Galilean port, who for private reasons now dwelt in Nazareth but still managed to practice their craft of boatbuilding. These, too, traveled down to the Sea of Galilee, often carrying bulkheads of timber and the like in low-sided carts drawn by oxen.

There was amongst the small and thriving community another craftsman who plied his trade diligently and with pride — one, a carpenter known as Joseph, whose espoused wife, Mary, was the mother of the boy Jesus, the same who had been born in a manger at Bethlehem.

The house of Joseph was close to that of the boatbuilders from Ptolemais, and his workshop adjacent to the neat and compact dwelling. Both the house and the workshop always had the sunlight, and yet, in the heat of the day, were cool because the buildings faced a gap in the hills through which the wind blew straight from off the distant Sea of Galilee.

On this morning when Petrus made a slow and painful journey down off the hills into the dusty village street, Joseph and Jesus were busy in the workshop repairing furniture for a neighbor.

But for the sounds of their activity, the village was exceedingly quiet, there being nobody about. One or two hens squatted in the shadows between the houses clucking contentedly and preening their feathers.

Petrus whimpered as he limped past the first of the houses, his ears closely pressed against his skull as if fearing what might happen to him in this place where men lived together and possibly possessed dogs of their own who might suddenly leap out on him and rend him.

Yet something drew Petrus on, despite the fear in his heart and the great weariness in his limbs. His eyes, piteous with longing, searched the alleys between the houses. There was nothing to molest him as he proceeded.

He heard the sound of activity from the carpenter's shop the instant he entered the village, and his attention was drawn toward it. His longing for companionship overwhelmed all other considerations. He was, at last, prepared to accept a master. Indeed, only one desire governed his every action, and that was to belong to someone as once before he had belonged. His awakening awareness of the past made him understand that there had indeed been a time when he had not been lonely and miserable as now, and to escape from that loneliness and misery he must yield his freedom to one prepared to accept it.

Because of that past which had molded so much of his

nature, he sensed that servitude was not a terrible thing. It brought one such as he great happiness — with the right master. . . .

Petrus limped steadily on, knowledge and understanding increasing in him with each step he took. What was most important, he sensed that soon his loneliness would be over, and the pain in his body and limbs smoothed away.

No fear had he when he stood at last outside the house of Joseph and Mary, staring in at the open door and listening to the ceaseless tapping in the workshop of tools shaping wood. Indeed, he was only conscious that beyond all the weariness and the pain, he had come after a long sojourn in strange places to the one spot where succor could be found.

Thus, there was no surprise in him when he beheld a certain woman coming from the house and pausing with surprise as she stared down at him.

Another miracle was granted him — the miracle of memory, complete, and without the slightest suggestion of darkness to distort the perfection of its image.

As Petrus looked up into the woman's face, despite the years that had gone by since that night in the stable at Bethlehem, he knew her, and she him. He saw in her eyes that same kindness and understanding that had been in them on that never-to-be-forgotten night when she had said to Saul: 'Be not angry with him. Do him no injury, for he, too, would look upon my Babe!'

Even as Petrus saw and understood the purport of her look, he suddenly beheld Saul also in his mind — Saul as he, too, had been on that night, and he seemed to hear once again the words the woman had uttered when she named him. . . . 'He should be called "Petrus" for his nose is cold like a stone that has lain long in the river. . . .'

All these things Petrus saw and understood as the past came vibrantly alive. Moreover, as on that wonderful night, the woman standing before him suddenly bent down, holding out her hand to him.

The dog moved forward slowly to sniff it, and somehow it was quite natural for him to hear her call him 'Petrus.'

Mary uttered the word softly and with great tenderness. She knew not with any degree of certainty why she called the animal Petrus save that the animal before her could only be the dog she had once known. Not a day older either, but so weary and travel-stained — and, in pain.

'Petrus,' she said again, and as she said it, she knew that it was indeed the very same dog, knew it without doubting the miracle that had brought him hence and preserved his youth so that she would know him from amongst a thousand others of his kind.

Suddenly she turned her head, calling out to Joseph and Jesus who were still in the workshop.

'Joseph! Jesus!' she cried. 'Come quickly!'

The activity in the workshop ceased, and two people came hastening out into the street to pause with surprise at Mary's side. One, bearded, and grown old with the years that were on him, was a direct contrast to the youth beside him who was upright and young, but with a face that held all power and wisdom and love.

'It is the dog Petrus,' Mary said slowly.

Joseph, remembering the animal of whom she spoke, looked down at the dog and shook his head.

'It cannot be,' he answered. 'This dog, despite his poor condition, is still young. Jesus, here, is nigh unto His fifteenth year. That dog, of whom you speak, must be dead these many years.'

Mary shook her head emphatically.

'It is the same who looked upon our Son when He was a Babe, and we in the stable at Bethlehem because there was no room for us at the inn. . . .'

The young man then stepped forward. He knelt before Petrus, passing His hands, gentle and yet strong, tenderly over the dog's body.

Petrus looked up into His face, and experienced such happiness and peace as he had never known before. Truly had he come to the end of his long journeying, and with it, the end of his long hour of despair.

He held up one paw.

Jesus took hold of it.

Then in compassion, He cried: 'He is hurt and in pain. See, his feet are blistered and broken.'

Before either Mary or Joseph could lend Him assistance, He had picked the dog up in His arms, and despite the animal's size, held him fast and carried him into the house.

Petrus, looking up into His face, knew that here was his Master, the one Master he must follow for the rest of his days. All things were made clear to the dog then. There was in him so much of understanding and so much of love. In the early morning and in the late night, through long year to yet another long year, through all joy and happiness, through all pain and the fear of death, Petrus, the dog whose nose was cold like a stone that had lain long in the river, would follow his Master, Jesus, until there could be no more following, and no more sunlight, and no more love. . . .

Thus was the long quest ended, and the dog, Petrus, bound forever to Jesus, His Master!

Legend of the Dog of Damascus

'. . . And when He had come nigh unto Damascus, He sought rest by the wayside, and those that were with Him, did likewise, the heat and burden of the day being wearisome.

'And there came to Him as He rested, a dog who had followed Him these many days: and lying beside Him, the dog did lick His feet which the heat had blistered. . . .'

AUTHOR'S NOTE

In this story of Petrus, I have sought to show that from time immemorial dogs have ever been the companions of man. Their singleness of purpose and devotion merit for them far better treatment than is often given to them by people who fail to understand that they, and indeed all animals, are creatures of feeling, and therefore suffer when badly used.

As a special tribute to all the dogs I have known and who have given me so much joy and happiness over the years, I would mention in particular

ORPAL, MAX, REX,
AND PETER,

also Rajah who, somehow, refuses to let me forget him.

JOSEPH E. CHIPPERFIELD